$\mathscr{A}$ snowball unexpectedly and painfully pounded hard into the back of my head. "Ow!"

Putting my hand back there, rubbing the sore spot, I spun around and could hardly believe my eyes. My irksome brother was standing on the wooden deck, a huge cocky grin plastered on his irritatingly handsome face.

"You're building a snowman? What are you, like, two years old?" he taunted.

I was stunned. My brain wouldn't function, no words would come forth. Because standing right beside him, grinning as well, was . . .

Tall, dark, and handsome Brad Connor.

# Love on the Lifts

## RACHEL HAWTHORNE

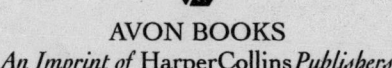

AVON BOOKS
*An Imprint of* HarperCollins*Publishers*

*To Terri, Renee, and Maggie*
*With Love*

# Love on the Lifts

# Chapter 1

"A totally hot ski instructor," Leah suddenly announced excitedly. "That's what you need to take your mind completely off Brad Connor."

"How can a ski instructor be *hot*?" I asked. "His classroom is a snow-covered hill. He's gotta be cold."

Allie rolled her eyes and Leah gave me a sharp look that said she was seriously contemplating throwing the snow she'd just scooped up at me.

"That is so lame, Kate."

Okay, so it *was* lame, but I was also extremely cold, with visions of curling up in front of a roaring fire dancing through my head. And obviously, the chill seeping through the knitted cap I'd pulled down over my ears was causing periodic brain freezes. Even stuffing my shoulder-length, obnoxiously naturally curly red hair under the cap didn't seem to provide any extra insulation against the frigid air that surrounded us.

And it was unbelievably cold. After all, we were in a ski resort town with white peaked mountains all around us.

Leah, Allie, and I had flown in earlier that afternoon. My aunt had met us at the airport and driven us to Snow Angel Valley where she'd made arrangements for us to stay in a condo by ourselves. It was totally awesome. Three bedrooms, a sunken living room, a redwood deck. But more importantly, it was ours for the duration of our visit. Just ours. No parents, no chaperones. We were totally on our own, with the freedom to do exactly what we wanted.

Once we'd settled into our respective bedrooms, Allie had announced that she wanted to build a snowman. But now that we were actually doing it, the activity seemed as lame as my joke. I mean, really, we were seniors, and a snowman is something you care about if you're, like, two years old—or if you've never been around snow.

Leah and Allie had never been around snow.

I saw it at least once a year, usually over winter break when I came to visit Aunt Sue while my parents took their annual gotta-get-away-from-it-all cruise down to the Bahamas. Aunt Sue lived in Snow Angel Valley, owned a bookstore-slash-hot chocolate café, and rented condos to the tourists more than she did to the locals. This winter break, remarkably, one of her condos wasn't being rented.

So she'd offered to let me stay in it instead of staying with her in her apartment over the bookstore. She owns all these nice condos, but she lives in an apartment. Go figure. She calls herself a minimalist, preferring a simple life to one "cluttered with materialistic objects that serve no purpose other than to provide a place for dust to gather." Her words, not mine.

But you gotta love someone who sees dusting and scrubbing as a poor use of one's time.

"I've never seen a headstone inscribed 'May she rest in peace. She kept a clean house.'"

Again, her words, not mine. Not that Aunt

Sue is a slob or anything. She's not. She simply doesn't believe in spending time doing things that aren't important to her.

She is absolutely, without question, one of the coolest people I know. Especially since she told me that I could bring along a couple of my friends to share the condo with me.

So I did. Leah Locke and Allie Anderson. And I'm Kate Kennedy. We call ourselves the alphabet trio because somehow we all ended up with our first and last names starting with the same letter. Alliteration. Of course, we have a lot more in common than our alliterating names.

We attend the same high school, live in the same neighborhood, have the same best friends (each other), and are presently boyfriendless.

Although I have to admit that I've been crushing on my brother's college roommate Brad Connor ever since Mom, Dad, and I went to the university to visit Sam during family weekend. That's when I met Brad. And oh my gosh, is he a hunk. Tall, dark, and handsome doesn't even begin to describe him. He has a killer smile —

"Why are we making our snowman round?" Leah asked, interrupting my nostalgic musings about Brad.

Beneath Leah's red cap, she has cropped hair that was brown until she dyed it as black as a raven's wing. It gives her a sort of goth look that gets her a lot of stares when we go out. Or maybe it's her stunningly beautiful violet eyes. Or her pierced eyebrow. Or her braided leather choker. She has this really dark, mysterious aura going on that doesn't really fit with her bubbly personality. She even designed this mosaic that she plans to have tattooed on her neck the day she turns eighteen. Me, I don't want needles anywhere near my jugular.

"Because that's the way snowmen are supposed to be," Allie said.

Allie, on the other hand, is the girl-next-door. She'd stuffed her blonde hair beneath her pink knitted cap. Her pink coat had fur around the cuffs and collar. She's Barbie-doll petite, which sometimes irritates Leah, since she only has to look at chocolate in order to absorb the calories. Fortunately for me, since

I'm a chocoholic, I was born with a high metabolism that burns calories quickly. That sometimes irritates Leah, too.

"How would you know how snowmen are supposed to be?" Leah asked.

"I've seen pictures," Allie retorted.

The part of Texas where we live had never been visited by a single snowflake, which was the reason they were so totally into building this snow guy.

Leah picked up a twig. "Let's be creative. Let's make him buff, give him some abs, some guns—"

"Guns? Are you going to make him a cowboy—" I began.

"No." Leah held her arm up at a right angle, closing her hand into a fist. "Guns. Muscled arms. That's what my brother calls them."

Her younger brother is on the football team and into working out. Not that he needed to work out. He was huge.

"Guess I don't know about guns, since Sam isn't into that whole being-in-shape thing. He's so incredibly skinny."

"He's not that skinny," Allie said.

"He's not buff, either."

"But our snowman should be," Leah said. "Otherwise, he's like everyone else's snowman, and what fun is that? Come on, let's put him on a diet and into a workout program."

She knelt in front of our lopsided snowman. He was really pitiful-looking, listing to the side a bit, all lumpy, not at all the way snowmen appeared in drawings that I'd seen in picture books when I was a kid.

"I think we can turn him into a sexy stud," Leah said.

"*You* can turn him into a sexy stud. I'm pretty sure I hear hot chocolate calling to me." Aunt Sue's shop had more than fifty varieties and was only a couple of blocks up the street.

"It won't take me that long. Let me finish before it gets dark. Tomorrow we'll be skiing and I might not be able to get back to him."

"I don't think he's going to melt anytime soon."

"I like to finish what I start."

That was true enough. I'd never known anyone as single-minded as Leah. I couldn't deny my best friend this one small pleasure.

Besides, like I said, she'd never been around snow. I wanted her to enjoy it as much as possible.

"Not a problem. The hot chocolate will wait," I told her, as I sat on the wooden steps that led up to the redwood deck.

The condo was situated on a hill, sloping down into the back. The lower level, what I considered the basement, wasn't completely underground. It had high windows that actually looked out on the backyard. From the street, we'd entered the second level of the house, which was considered the main area and contained the sunken living room, a kitchen, and a bedroom. If we walked through the main room, we came to the sliding glass doors that led out to the deck, where water from the hot tub steamed up to create a foggy mist.

Why anyone would need a hot tub during the winter was beyond me, but there you have it. All the condos on this street had steam rising from hot tubs. I had yet to see anyone use one. A waste of electricity keeping the water heated, as far as I was concerned.

We'd gone through the sliding glass door

and down the steps to play in the backyard. To build our snowman. Like little kids.

So much snow had fallen before we got here that our booted feet sunk into it when we walked over the ground. It covered the deck and the steps. Which was good. You want lots of snow—powder—when you're going skiing.

I tucked my gloved hands into the pockets of my parka and watched as Leah began scraping away some of the snow that we'd worked so hard to gather up for our creation.

She stopped and glanced over her shoulder. "So what do you think about what I said? Let's find you a ski instructor."

There was that single-minded purpose of hers.

Both Leah and Allie, by virtue of being my best friends, knew about my crush. They also knew that he looked through me like I was an open window.

I wrinkled my cold nose. At least I think I wrinkled it. It was frigid, almost numb. "I don't know. I really like Brad. Going after a ski instructor seems a little bit like being unfaithful."

"But he hardly knows you exist," Leah pointed out.

"True, but a ski instructor would be temporary—"

"Which is why he would be so perfect. No long-term commitment. Just short-term fun!"

"I think Leah's idea is fantastic!" Allie exclaimed. "We spend the time while we're here honing our flirtation skills. Then when you tell your brother that each of us was heavily involved with someone over winter break—"

"Why would I tell Sam that *all* of us were involved with someone?"

Looking down, Allie stomped the toe of her white boot against the snow, creating a hole. "I don't know. He might want to know what all of us did. Or you could just tell him about your experiences. My point being"—she lifted her gaze back to mine—"that when Sam tells Brad that you had a guy chasing after you, Brad's interest will skyrocket and he'll be all about getting to know you."

"Do you really think that Sam—not knowing that I have a crush on Brad—is going to tell Brad anything at all about what I do? Guys are not like girls. They talk about dumb stuff, like who is the best NFL quarterback and where can they find a handy poker tournament. They don't try to figure out how they can get together with someone."

"Maybe you should tell Sam how you feel about his roommate," Allie said. "Maybe he'd invite Brad to come home with him on the weekends."

"Right. Like Sam is going to care. He thinks I'm just his stupid baby sister."

"You think he's your stupid older brother, so it all works out," Leah said, backing up a little to inspect the snowman's abs.

I had to admit he was starting to look pretty good. Not a surprise really. Leah is heavy into art, and sculpting is her thing. That and designing tattoos.

"Because he *is* stupid," I said, responding to her comment about Sam. "He treats me like a kid, even though he's only a year older than me."

"But he's in college—" Allie began.

"So? I'll be in college next year. Besides, he's always treated me like I'm just a kid. I can't tell him anything personal or important. I especially can't tell him anything like 'I think your roommate is God's gift to girls.' He'd make my life impossible."

"Brad *is* cute," Leah said.

Under the pretense of wanting to record the history of my brother's year at college, I'd asked to take a picture of Sam with his roommate. Unfortunately, the zoom on my digital camera had somehow been pressed—by a renegade finger, I assumed—and I'd only been able to get a really good close-up shot of Brad. No evidence of Sam in sight. Gosh, darn. What a shame!

The photo was now the background wallpaper on my computer desktop.

"His eyes are so incredibly blue. It's like looking into a vast sky." I sighed. "I could look into them all day, all night."

"His whole package is good-looking," Leah said. "Kinda like our snowman now."

I smiled. "He is looking good."

"Are you talking about the snowman or Brad?"

"Both." She'd given the snowman abs, a chest, and upper arms—guns.

Leah tossed aside his rock eyes and his pencil nose — we hadn't been able to find a carrot. Aunt Sue had stocked the fridge and pantry for us, but she obviously hadn't expected us to undertake creating a snowman, us being seniors and all. Hence, no carrot.

"Who should I make him look like?" Leah asked.

"Kate's Brad," Allie said.

"He's not my Brad."

"He could be if you'd practice on a ski instructor," Leah said.

"I don't know. It sounds so . . . tawdry."

"And that's a problem because . . ."

She left the question dangling on the air, waiting for me to come up with a good excuse.

"Look, it doesn't hurt to kiss a few frogs before finally kissing your prince," she added, tired of waiting for me.

"Are you going to flirt with a ski instructor?" I asked.

"You bet."

I looked at Allie. "Are you?"

It was difficult to tell because she was so bundled up but I think she shrugged. "I guess.

What can it hurt? Besides, I could use a little romance in my life."

"I think we all can," Leah said. "After all, we'll be here for three whole weeks. We might as well have someone hot to cuddle against and keep us warm."

"All right. I'm game if y'all are," I said. I didn't want to be the only one without someone to snuggle with.

"Great!" Leah pointed her gloved finger at our buff snowman. "Okay, back to the really important issue. Who should I make him look like?"

Leah is like that. Carrying on two or three conversations at once. Sometimes she makes my head spin.

"Well, if Kate doesn't want it to be Brad, how about Colin Farrell," Allie suggested.

"All right. Let's pack some more snow on his head so I have enough to work with," Leah instructed.

Reaching down I scooped up a handful of snow. I shoved myself up from the steps, walked over to the snowman, and patted the snow into the ball on top of his body.

"I've seen some pictures of awesome ice sculptures," I said. "In Alaska or somewhere. Every year they create all these fantastic sculptures."

"I'd love to do something like that," Leah said. "Maybe I'll create a garden of snow sculptures while I'm here."

"Well, you have plenty of snow to work with." I glanced off into the distance. The mountains were beautiful, covered in glistening white.

"We'll be on the mountains tomorrow," I told them. "I can't wait."

A snowball unexpectedly and painfully pounded hard into the back of my head. "Ow!"

Putting my hand back there, rubbing the sore spot, I spun around and could hardly believe my eyes. My irksome brother was standing on the wooden deck, a huge cocky grin plastered on his irritatingly handsome face.

Why had I gotten stuck with the red hair and freckles like Mom while he had not a freckle in sight and had inherited Dad's dark hair? I tried to take consolation in the fact that he wouldn't hold on to that beautiful thick hair forever. Eventually, hopefully, it would start to disappear like Dad's was now doing.

"You're building a snowman? What are you, like, two years old?" he taunted.

I was stunned. My brain wouldn't function, no words would come forth. Because standing right beside him, grinning as well, was . . .

Brad Connor.

# Chapter 2

"*You're* one to talk," I finally tossed back at him when my brain kicked into gear. "Throwing snowballs. What are you, like, one?"

Okay, so maybe my brain was still in lockdown mode. It was trying to putter along, but it obviously wasn't warmed up yet.

"God, Kate, your comebacks are sharp enough to . . . well, heck, I guess they aren't sharp."

Nothing more humiliating than having someone point out the obvious, especially in front of someone you like. I glowered at Sam. "What are you doing here, anyway?"

"Aunt Sue invited me and my buds to use the condo over winter break."

My mouth dropped open. "Not *this* condo!"

"Yeah, *this* condo."

"But we're using it."

"We can share. You remember my roommate, Brad, right?"

Since he made a nightly appearance in my dreams and was plastered all over my computer screen at home, yeah, I remembered him.

"Hey, Brad," I said.

He leaned forward, folded his arms on the railing, and gave me a smile that could have melted our snowman, because it was sure melting me. "Hey."

I didn't think I'd ever heard one word sound so incredible. He made it seem so important, and I know I was probably grinning like an idiot, but I couldn't help it.

"And this is Joe Foster," Sam said.

My mother had raised me to be polite. I tore my gaze from Brad "the hunk" Connor and shot a quick glance at the grinning guy standing on the other side of Sam. "Hi."

"Cool snowman."

"Thanks. Going the nontraditional route was Leah's idea." With my thumbs, I pointed to my friends standing on either side of me.

"Leah and Allie."

"Hey, Sam," Allie said, sounding a little breathless. Cold could do that to you. "Brad, Joe."

The guys muttered their greetings, but Brad's gaze never wandered from me. I was completely down with having him stay in the condo, but no way did I want Sam around. I would be too self-conscious flirting with Brad while Sam looked on. Especially since I knew Sam would give me a hard time about it once he realized I had a serious interest in Brad. It's just the way Sam was.

Besides, we'd gotten here first and staked our claim. After all, this area of Colorado used to be mining country, and that was the way it was done. You staked your claim. Let Sam find someplace else to bed down.

I forced my attention back to him. "You can't stay here. There are only three bedrooms, and we've already claimed them."

Sam held up a finger. "There's the main bedroom on this level—"

"I'm familiar with the bedrooms. We've already checked them out and settled in. That one is mine." Although it had a king-size bed in it, I wasn't about to share it with anyone. Okay, not completely true. I could see myself sharing it with Brad, but not if Sam was around.

"—two bedrooms at the level below," Sam continued as though I hadn't spoken, holding up two more fingers like he was talking to a kindergartener. "Each has a set of bunk beds. That's five beds." He flashed five fingers. "And the couch. Six people, six places to sleep. We can work it out."

"Sam could sleep in my room if he wanted," Allie said quietly.

"*Please*! He snores and has stinky feet. He can stay with Aunt Sue. She invited him."

"Kate, this is non-negotiable." Sam liked to throw around words like that, like he was always in charge, just because he was fifteen months older. Another reason I didn't want him around. He thought he was the boss of me. I didn't want Brad to see me as a kid. He'd lose all interest.

"We're staying," Sam continued. "And it's childish to deny us a bed when they're available."

It was childish. I knew it was and his pointing it out made me seem even more childish. At that moment I hated my brother, but I tried to look on the bright side. Brad hadn't taken his eyes off me and he was still grinning. I just didn't know if he was grinning because he liked watching me or he thought I was having a totally moronic conversation with my brother. Where was my confidence when I needed it?

"Allie can move into my room," Leah said. "I'll even let her choose the upper or lower bunk. That'll leave one whole bedroom for the guys to use."

Okay, this could work if Brad took the couch. He'd be upstairs with me while every-one else—

"I'll take the couch," Joe said, and I hoped my face didn't reflect my disappointment.

"Great!" Sam said. "We're all set then. We'll haul in our stuff and leave you girls to finish playing with your snowman."

Sam was still chortling like one of the three stooges as the guys disappeared into the condo. I wanted to kick my brother for his arrogance and for always making me feel so stupid. Frustrated, I spun around and drove my booted foot into our snowman.

"Hey!" Leah said, slapping at my leg. "Don't destroy my creation just because you want to destroy your brother. Besides, this is great!"

Had her brain totally frozen in the cold?

"What's so great about it?"

"*Brad*?" She gave me a pointed look. "Staying with us, sleeping with us, eating with us."

I shook my head. "Not with Sam here, too. You see how he treats me."

"Forget about Sam. Focus on Brad. You wanted him to notice you. This is the perfect opportunity for you to get to know him. And better yet, for him to get to know you. No ski instructor for you, girlfriend. You get to have the real thing!"

"I can't believe you invited Sam. And I can't believe you didn't tell me that you'd invited him."

Leah might have thought our present situation was great, but I was not yet convinced. Not as long as Sam was in the picture. I'd trudged down the hill to the main part of the village where my aunt had her bookstore—A Novel Place.

"Katie, sweetie, I couldn't make the offer to use the condo to you and not to him," Aunt Sue said.

"Sure you could have," I muttered.

"Besides, I thought I told you he'd be here," she said, totally ignoring my previous statement.

"No, I would have remembered if you'd told me something as horrible as sharing the condo with my brother."

I was sitting on a stool at the hot chocolate counter, sipping on some comforting mint chocolate. My mug matched Aunt Sue's. It showed the backs of four cowboys sitting on a fence and below them was written HOT BUNS AND COCOA TO START THE DAY. Like Leah with the snowman, Aunt Sue appreciated the fine shape of a man.

In addition to the hot chocolate counter and the bookstore area, A Novel Place also had a little area in the front where people could curl up in plush chairs or on loveseats with a book and something warm to drink. It drew in the crowds when it was really cold outside, which was at least half the year.

A fire was dancing in the corner fireplace nearby, the scent of burning cedar filling the air. The huge window looked out over the town and the mountains. It was a breathtaking view.

Aunt Sue placed her elbows on the counter and leaned toward me, her long gray braid draped over her shoulder. She's always reminded me of a gypsy, a free spirit, the complete opposite of my mom even though they're sisters. She has dark green eyes like mine, and in her youth, her hair had been the same shade of red as mine. She still had freckles. Unfortunately, so did I.

While working in the store, she dressed in flowing clothes so the exact shape of her body seemed a mystery. That was how I always thought of her — as a mystery.

She lived in Snow Angel Valley during the winter months when business was brisk. But in summer when there weren't many tourists, she closed down everything and traveled the world, going to . . . well, going to *novel* places.

I hadn't been sure if she'd named her shop A Novel Place because it was a place where novels were kept or if the name referred to the places she'd visited and the photos she'd hung on the walls. There were framed pictures of herself with Sherpas at the bottom of Mount Everest, penguins in Antarctica, kangaroos in Australia—too many photos to list them all. My aunt had set foot on all seven continents and swam in all the oceans. She wanted to travel on the space shuttle someday.

She was an adventurer and I loved her dearly. When I'd once asked her what the name of the shop applied to—the books or the places she'd been—she'd said, "A Novel Place means many things on different levels. It's a state of mind."

Thoughts too heavy for me to figure out. But I loved her anyway. Even though I was presently majorly ticked off at her.

"What's wrong, Katie?" she asked. "You're not upset because your brother is here. There's more to it than sharing space with Sam; since you've done that most of your life. So let's get to the root of the problem so we can address it and you can have a good time while you're here."

She knew me too well, and I knew I could trust her with anything.

"It's Brad," I admitted reluctantly.

"Sam's roommate?"

Scrunching up my face, my nose no longer numb thanks to the hot mist of chocolate tickling it while I drank, I nodded dejectedly.

"What's wrong with him?" she asked.

"That's the problem. There's nothing wrong with him."

"I see," she said, drawing out the last word like she wanted to savor it. "He *is* a cutie."

I've never known Aunt Sue to think any guy *wasn't* a cutie. Not even the ancient hunched-over village mailman who looked like he'd been born around the time the mountains were carved by glaciers.

"He's such a cutie," she'd say after handing him complimentary hot chocolate to-go when he stopped by to deliver her mail twice a day. On really cold days, he delivered mail to her three or four times. Always junk mail that I thought he held in reserve for emergency deliveries, but she'd act like she was thrilled to get it as she handed him his hot chocolate to-go.

"When did you see Brad?" I asked, turning my thoughts back to my immediate concern and impending nightmare.

"Sam and his friends stopped by to pick up a key to the condo. I thought Joe was cute, too."

"Joe?"

"His other friend?"

Oh, yeah. The sandy blond–haired guy who had also been standing on the balcony smiling. Was he cute? I couldn't really draw an impression of him from my memory except for the smile. It was pretty dazzling as I recalled, but nothing at all like Brad's. Brad was the hottie of the group, hands down. No competition there whatsoever. And like I said, Aunt Sue thought every guy was cute, so I'd really have to take another gander at Joe to properly assess his cuteness factor.

"Oh, yeah, right," I mumbled. "Joe."

"So Brad is the one for you, huh?"

I nodded again.

"Well, then. This is the perfect opportunity for him to get to know you better."

"But if Sam notices that I'm crushing on his roommate, he will tease me unmercifully — and he'll do it in front of Brad. I know he will.

It'll be a major turnoff for Brad. Sam will ruin everything. And I like Brad so much."

"Why?"

I stared at her. "You've seen him."

"Yep. Like I said, he's a cutie. And I've talked to him, and he's nice. But I need more than cute and nice to give a guy my heart."

"What else do you need?"

She winked, before turning to help a customer, and tossing over her shoulder back at me, "That's what *you* have to figure out."

# Chapter 3

"Okay, we need to talk house rules," I announced.

Sam was lounging on the couch, Brad and Joe were sitting in the recliners, all were watching a football game.

"Later, Katie, we're busy," Sam said, never taking his eyes from the thirty-six–inch screen.

I walked over to the TV and turned it off. That got an immediate reaction. Sam bolted upright, his feet hitting the floor with a resounding thud.

"Hey! Brady was about to throw a pass!"

Tom Brady of the New England Patriots. I'll admit he was cute enough to get my attention, but I'd never tell my brother that. Or that I knew most of his quarterback stats.

"I'll turn on the TV—" I began.

Sam picked up the remote, clicked a button, and the echo of screaming fans filled the room.

"Sam!"

"Later, Kate. You made us miss the touchdown. Now move your butt so I can see the game."

"Hey, man, relax."

This from Joe, who'd put the footrest down on his recliner and was now sitting up as well. "She wasn't expecting us to invade her space, so let her give us the rules."

Joe didn't seem at all bothered by the glower Sam threw at him. Then Sam looked over at Brad.

Brad shrugged. "Whatever, dude."

Sam leaned back and stretched his arm across the back of the couch, like some emperor giving his subjects an audience or something. "Okay then, let's discuss the rules."

Could he get any more irritating?

"Mute the TV," I ordered.

To my surprise he clicked the remote again, and the TV fell silent. No arguments from him. Thank goodness.

Allie and Leah came to stand beside me, the three of us forming a united front. I looked down at my yellow legal pad. We'd held an impromptu meeting in my bedroom to discuss our demands, so we'd be prepared when facing the guys.

Allie didn't see the need for rules. She trusted Sam and his friends to be good roomies. But I knew Sam a lot better than she did, and Leah had two brothers—so Leah and I knew a little more about living with guys than Allie did, since she had only one sister. We definitely needed rules.

"Rule number one: Toilet seats are to be placed in the down position before exiting the bathroom."

Sam rolled his eyes and groaned. "Kate—"

"It's non-negotiable."

I heard a snicker of laughter from Joe. Sam looked over at him. Joe was shaking his head, grinning. He did have a cute smile.

"Hey, man, I've got three sisters," Joe said to Sam. "You're not going to win this one."

"Fine, Kate, you can have your rule." Sam snapped his fingers impatiently at me. "What else?"

I felt a surge of triumph. Gosh, it felt good. I seldom won an argument with Sam. I looked back at my list. "Rule number two: The girls will cook if the guys will clean."

"Sure, I've got no problem washing my hands before I eat. I'm civilized."

Honestly, my brother was totally clueless sometimes.

"Not clean your hands, stupid. The kitchen. We want you to clean the kitchen, the pots, the pans, the counters. We spend time cooking, you spend time cleaning, fair trade."

Sam looked at Brad, who was nodding. Joe, too. Sam looked back at me. "How many meals will you cook?"

"We'll fix breakfast and dinner. For lunch we'll be on the slopes so we'll all fend for our-selves."

"There's a dishwasher in there, right?"

"Yes, but you have to rinse the food off before you put the dishes in it."

Sam nodded. "Like I said, I'm not totally uncivilized. What else?"

I didn't quite trust the ease with which he'd capitulated, but decided to trust him for now.

"We—meaning Allie, Leah, and I—get the TV for two hours every night, the exact times to be decided by us."

"No way! We're in the middle of the play-offs!"

"Exactly. Which is the reason we want some TV time."

"Nope. Ain't gonna happen. It's non-negotiable."

"It's football! As long as you see the end of the game, why do you have to see the beginning? The end is when it gets exciting. That's what you really want to see."

"And what is it you want to watch, Kate? Some girly—"

"*Lost*, for starters."

"I'm down with that," Joe said. "I'm hooked on that show."

I shot a quick look over at Joe. He was still smiling, an unexpected ally in this war.

"It's childish to hog the TV, Sam," I said. "And selfish."

Sam narrowed his eyes at me. He didn't like having his words tossed back at him. Too bad. He shouldn't have thrown a snowball earlier. I still owed him for that and was already plotting my revenge. I planned to get him where it would hurt him the most.

"Okay, you can have your two hours, but it can't be during the last hour of a game."

I looked at Allie and Leah. They both nodded. I turned my attention back to Sam. "Okay."

Sam sighed. "Next."

I looked at my list, looked back up. "That's it."

"Okay." Sam gave me a familiar grin. I knew it too well. It said I was in trouble.

"*The guys'* rules. No girly things hanging in the bathroom to dry. The guys get the bathrooms first in the morning because we're fast and efficient. If you want to hitch a ride with us to the slopes, you have to be ready to leave when we are. We're not waiting for you. When the guys are watching football, the girls can't be in here talking—"

"Whoa! There's this room, the kitchen, and our bedrooms. You can't not share this room with us."

"She's right, dude," Brad said. "I don't mind having the babes around. I mean I like football, but I like having babes around more, you know what I'm saying?"

"Yeah, but one of the babes isn't your sister," Sam said.

Brad winked at me, while talking to Sam. "All the better, dude."

My heart did this little somersaulting flutter inside my chest. Had Leah and Aunt Sue been right? Was this the perfect opportunity to have Brad fall for me as much as I'd already fallen for him? Had I misjudged the Sam factor?

I was almost giddy as I turned my attention back to Sam, ready to be more than magnanimous. "What other rules do you have?"

"That's it."

I breathed a huge sigh of relief. That had gone a lot easier than I'd expected.

"I'll add your rules to ours, then we can all sign—"

"Kate, we don't have to sign anything. We've agreed to the rules. Now move away from the TV. The Pats are back in scoring position."

"You're from Texas. You're supposed to like the Cowboys or the Texans."

"I like anyone who's good. And the rule is you don't talk when we're watching football, so"—

he made a zipping motion across his mouth —
"go."

"I still think we should sign —"

"We're not signing. It's non-negotiable."

"If he doesn't follow a rule, I'll kick his butt,"
Joe said, still smiling warmly.

I couldn't figure out what color his eyes
were. Were they brown or green? A light blue?

"Yeah, Mr. Law and Order over here will
make sure all the rules are followed," Sam said.
"Now, Kate, please get out of the way before I
haul you to the deck and toss you into the snow."

"I'd like to see you try," was what I heard
inside my head, but since Brad was sitting
there, I didn't give actual voice to the words.
That, too, was a disadvantage to having Sam
around. I'd have to fight my natural inclination
to constantly argue with him. Who wanted a
shrew for a girlfriend? Plus I didn't want to
appear childish again. I took a deep breath.
"Only because you said please."

With my shoulders squared, I walked away
from the TV with Allie and Leah following
behind me.

We'd won. Sorta.

"Did you see the way Brad looked at you?" Leah asked. "Too cool!"

We'd retreated to my bedroom. As soon as the door was closed, I'd done the happy dance around the room before plopping on the quilt-covered king-size sleigh bed. This room was totally romantic, and I was feeling very romanced—in a subtle kind of way.

"Did you see Brad wink?" I asked. "He actually winked at me. Have you ever seen anything so sexy?"

"It was definitely hot," Allie said. "And directed entirely at you. It was like Leah and I weren't even there. He wants you around, Kate. That's so great, especially since it's incredibly obvious that Sam *doesn't* want us around."

"My brother can be such a jerk. Is it any wonder that he can't get a girlfriend?"

"He's not that bad," Leah said. "You should try living with my brothers sometime."

"No thanks."

"Honestly, guys, I don't think it's that Sam doesn't want us around," Leah said. "It's like Joe said. We weren't expecting them; they might not have been expecting us. So we make the best of the situation."

"You're right," Allie said. "And the best of the situation is that Brad has a definite interest in Kate."

"The best is that the guys will clean the kitchen," Leah said, grinning. "I hate cleaning the kitchen."

"Who doesn't?" I asked. Maybe my mom. Nah, I was pretty sure she hated it, too.

"Speaking of the guys," Leah said, "I gotta confess, Joe is to die for. The way he looked at you, Kate, while you were reading off our demands—so intense. Like he was really listening, really cared. And the way he took our side was totally awesome. My brothers would walk barefoot over glass before they'd side with me on anything."

"He surprised me, jumping to our defense the way he did," I admitted. "You're welcome to him." Grimacing, I looked over at Allie. "But if we pair up, me with Brad, Leah with Joe, that would leave you with Sam. I wouldn't foist my brother off on my worst enemy. I guess we better not try to pair up."

"No, way!" Leah said. "Operation Get-Brad-Together-With-Kate is officially underway. Allie and I can take turns with the other two, so there's no obvious pairing, except for you and Brad."

"But if you're interested in Joe . . ." Allie's voice trailed off.

"I'm not interested in him as a potential winter break boyfriend or anything," Leah said. "I just think he's cute. Our real goal here is to get Brad with Kate. And if Allie and I have to play guy-tag for that to happen, so be it. No hardship."

I nibbled on my bottom lip, trying not to get too excited about the prospect that I might actually end my winter break with the boyfriend of my dreams.

"Are you guys sure you don't mind?"

"We're sure," Allie and Leah said at the same time.

"You guys are the absolute best."

"Of course we are," Leah said. "So what are we gonna cook for supper tonight?"

I groaned. "Right. I know Aunt Sue loaded the fridge and pantry for us, so there is bound to be something we can whip together. There's also a crock pot. We could fill it with something before we leave for the slopes in the morning. Let it simmer all day so it's ready when we get home."

"You mean like a stew?" Allie asked.

"Yeah. Or chili. We don't have to get fancy. Just so there's plenty of it and it's hot."

My cell phone began to chirp. I hopped off the bed, grabbed the backpack I'd left by the dresser earlier after I'd settled in, dug out my cell phone, and immediately recognized the number.

"Hey, Aunt Sue. Were you calling to make sure we still had survivors over here?"

She laughed. "This could be a reality show. A brother and sister snowed in together. How long can they survive?"

"No, thanks."

"But you did get everything worked out?"

"Pretty much, yeah."

"Good. Since you're all still alive and friends—"

"I wouldn't go that far."

She laughed again. My aunt had a really fun

laugh. Boisterous, like she enjoyed life. Which she did.

"How about we all get together for dinner tonight? My treat," she said.

Saved from cooking! "That would be great. Where did you have in mind?"

# Chapter 4

$P$ile It On Pizza was where we all ended up. Like every other restaurant and shop in Snow Angel Valley, it was quaint with its own unique atmosphere. Very rustic, it looked like the inside of a log cabin. We picked the size crust that we wanted, then we walked down the long length of the counter pointing to the ingredients we wanted piled on.

We ended up ordering two pizzas because the guys made a big production of groaning when Allie pointed to the green olives. My brother had always been a meat-and-potatoes-only kind of guy. I guess the others were as well.

They went with pepperoni, sausage, hamburger, and Canadian bacon. Aunt Sue, Allie, Leah, and I chose mushrooms, green olives, black olives, and more mushrooms. Pile It On honored its name. The guy at the counter piled it on until we told him to stop. Then into the oven they went.

We took two pitchers of root beer to a long wooden table. Allie, Leah, and even Aunt Sue, jockeyed for chairs at the table until miraculously, somehow, Brad ended up sitting beside me. Aunt Sue was at the head of the table, with Joe beside her, then Leah and Sam. Allie sat across from Sam, Brad was between Allie and me, and I was beside Aunt Sue. It couldn't have worked out better, except of course, for poor Allie who was stuck at the far end of the table across from my brother. I was afraid if she spent too much time with him she might re-evaluate her friendship with me. Was it worth putting up with Sam?

I glanced down there and saw that Sam was actually being polite, smiling, and talking with her. That was something that I didn't see very often—Sam being pleasant. Of course, I also didn't see him with my friends too often. He tended to avoid us like the plague.

"It's supposed to snow again tonight," Aunt

Sue said. "Fresh powder will make your ski experience so much better."

"Do you ski?" Joe asked.

Aunt Sue smiled. "Not as much as I used to. I fancy ski boarding these days and snowmobiling."

"A lot of people think snowmobiles are bad for the environment," I said. "The exhaust pollutes the wilderness and the noise disturbs the wildlife."

"That's true," Aunt Sue said. "But how else can one appreciate the undisturbed wilderness except by disturbing it a little bit? And once you get deep into the woods, away from town, turn off the engines . . . it is so humbling."

"Humbling?" Brad asked.

I loved the deep rumble of his voice. It just sorta went through me and I couldn't help but think about how heavenly it would be to have him whispering in my ear.

"It's incredibly quiet," Aunt Sue said. "A snow-hushed world. You can almost hear the snowflakes fall."

Brad drew his heavy dark brows together. "Snowflakes make noise?"

"She's being poetic," Joe said. "Not literal."

Brad shrugged, reached for the pitcher, and poured himself some more root beer. He nudged his shoulder against mine. "Want some?"

"Yeah." I held out my mug, smiled when he smiled at me. We were, like, so totally bonding.

When he finished pouring, he set the pitcher down, took a sip of his root beer, and focused his intense gaze on me. "What do you do for fun?" he asked.

And suddenly we weren't at a table with a large group of people anymore. It was just Brad and me. We'd moved from a wink to a nudge to a discussion, but his interest was going to disappear if I didn't think of something exciting to share.

"I like to read mysteries."

"Read."

He repeated the word like I'd just told him that I enjoyed stepping in dog poop.

I nodded, trying not to reveal that I was rattled that we didn't share an interest in reading and that he might be ranking me pretty high on the boring-ometer scale.

"I also meditate," I offered.

"What? Like yoga?"

"Yeah. Focusing on my breathing, the center of my being. I can teach you how."

He gave me this really wicked grin that set my heart to racing. "I know how to breathe." He leaned closer and I could smell whatever cologne he used. It was sharp and tangy. "And I know the center of my being."

"Of course you do." Think, Kate, think. Now is the time to be witty and clever.

Our number was called. Aunt Sue pointed to the guys. "You guys go grab the pizzas and two more pitchers of root beer."

As soon as they were far enough away not to notice, I tapped the heel of my hands against my forehead. "I am so lame!"

Reaching out, Aunt Sue rubbed my shoulder. "Katie, sweetie, relax."

"I can't think of anything interesting to say—after y'all went to so much trouble to make sure I was sitting beside him."

"It wasn't any trouble, Kate," Leah said. "Besides, Sam's entertaining us."

Great. My brother was an entertainer and I was a sleeping pill.

"Just be yourself, Kate," Aunt Sue said.

"Right. Right." I could do that.

The guys returned with the pizzas and root beer. As soon as Brad sat down, I said, "I love pizza."

Laughing loudly, he reached for a piece loaded with so much meat that I couldn't see the cheese. "Me, too."

I cheered up considerably. I'd made him laugh, and he was still looking at me as he munched his pizza.

"What do you like to do for fun?" I asked.

He chewed, swallowed. "Drive fast, kiss babes, ski."

Okay, I so didn't want to get into a discussion about him kissing babes, even though I hoped before winter break was over that I would end up being one that he'd kissed. So I went for something safe.

"You know how to ski?"

"Yeah, don't you?"

"Oh, yeah. I just thought maybe you were like Allie and Leah. They've never even seen snow. That's why we were building—well, actually *they* were building, I was just watching—the snowman." I really didn't want him to see me as a kid, the way Sam did.

"I've done some skiing," he reassured me. "I'm not planning to spend much time on the bunny slope."

The bunny slope was for beginners. Pretty much a simple short incline where you learned to keep your balance and bring yourself to a stop.

"I haven't hung out at the bunny slope in ages," I said.

"Cool. Maybe we can—"

"Excuse me. Sue? I thought that was you."

The woman interrupted our conversation, not so much because of her loud voice, but because Brad was suddenly staring past me like he'd just seen a Dallas Cowboys' cheerleader waving her pom-poms in his face. I desperately wanted to know what he was going to suggest that he and I do together. But other than clapping my hands in front of his nose, I didn't know how to get his attention, so I turned toward the voice, and realized my assessment of the person that went with it was right on.

The woman was tall, wearing stretch leggings

and a big red bulky sweater. Even though it was thick, it left no doubt that she filled it out a lot better than I filled out mine. Dolly Parton to my . . . well, let's just say that the greatly endowed wagon had passed me by. Her blonde hair was cascading in glorious waves around her shoulders instead of hanging in tight curls like mine. She no doubt knew her way around a curling iron.

She was resting a hand on Aunt Sue's shoulder like they were the very best of friends. I couldn't explain it, but I took an immediate dislike to her. Probably because Brad couldn't take his eyes off her and was starting to drool.

"Hey, everyone, this is Cynthia," Aunt Sue announced, like we all should care when I definitely did not. "She's staying at the condo next to yours. This is my niece, Kate, my nephew, Sam, and their friends."

"It's great to meet you all," Cynthia said a little too breathlessly, her voice having a little squeal to it, like she was trying really hard to sound sexy but she just came across sounding like a cat whose tail had been stepped on.

She leaned down closer to Aunt Sue. "I'm

sorry to bother you, Sue, but when I saw you sitting over here I thought I might as well take advantage of the opportunity to speak to you. I'm having trouble getting my garbage disposal to work. I was hoping you could send a maintenance guy over first thing tomorrow."

Before Aunt Sue could even open her mouth, Brad piped in with, "I can look at it tonight. I'm good with my hands."

Cynthia smiled. "I'll just bet you are. Are you sure you wouldn't mind?"

"Hell, no."

"I hate to disturb your evening."

"No problem."

He came out of his chair with so much force that I was surprised he didn't start an avalanche. Cynthia wound her arm around his and snuggled up against him.

"Lead the way, Cynthia," Brad said, this really goofy, stupid smile on his face.

As they were walking away, I heard Cynthia say, "My friends call me Cyn. I have a feeling you're about to become one of my friends."

"I wonder if she spells that S-I-N," I muttered.

I wanted to stick my finger down my throat and gag. Disappointment, hard and heavy, slammed into me as I watched them disappear out the door. Brad had been talking to me, had been on the verge of asking me to do something with him. It wasn't fair that someone else had come along and lured him away so effortlessly.

I think that's what hurt the most. All she'd had to do was show up at our table.

I turned my attention back to the pizza, my appetite gone. To make the situation more unbearable, I discovered Joe watching me. He had a funny look on his face. Sympathy maybe, like he knew I had a serious crush on Brad. And worse, he recognized that the guy had just stomped on my heart.

# Chapter 5

$\mathcal{I}$ couldn't sleep. My mind kept replaying my stupid banter — or lack thereof — during dinner and the quickness with which Brad had forgotten that I existed. The reality hurt.

And what made it even worse was that he hadn't come home by the time everyone had trudged off to bed at eleven, after watching another football game. It was now midnight. And I was starting to worry about him. I'd be able to get a good clear view of Cynthia's house from the deck. If the lights were still on, that meant they were still up. I really, really wanted them to be awake. I didn't want to contemplate that he was sleeping over there, sleeping with her. He'd just met her. I couldn't lose him completely, that quickly. There had to be other reasons that he hadn't come home.

For all I knew Brad was out there some-where, freezing to death, stretched out in the snow between the condos. Unnoticed.

Unlikely, but it could happen. What if he'd been knocking and no one heard him? Joe could be a sound sleeper or a loud snorer. I should have let Joe have the bed tonight, and I should have taken the couch so I could keep a vigil for Brad.

After all, how long could it take to fix a garbage disposal? He could have built her a freaking new one by now. With his teeth.

I got out of bed, grabbed my thick blue fleece robe that I always brought with me to Snow Angel Valley, drew it tightly around me, tied the sash, and slipped into my fuzzy slip-pers. Gingerly, as quietly as possible, I opened my door and peered out.

All the lights were off, but the TV was on and a fire was blazing in the gas fireplace. Gas wasn't as romantic as the real log fireplace that Aunt Sue had in her store, but it wasn't as much work either. Flip a switch, and we had a fire. No messing with kindling and setting logs up just right.

I walked out of my bedroom and down the four steps into the sunken part of the living room.

Wearing sweat pants and a T-shirt, his arms folded across his chest, Joe was sitting on the couch, his bare feet resting on the coffee table. My first thought was that they had to be cold. My next thought was that he had large feet. But then most guys did.

He must have heard me approach because he looked over his shoulder. "Sorry. Is the TV too loud?"

"No, I just . . ." I pulled hard on my sash and looked toward the front door, hoping Brad would walk through it at any second. I was at a loss for words, wondering what excuse I could give Joe to explain why I wanted to step out onto the deck at midnight.

"He's not back yet," Joe said.

Maybe no excuse was needed. I turned my attention back to Joe, who was watching me with that same intensity that he had at Pile It On Pizza.

"I don't know how he'll get in. He doesn't

have a key, but I guess you'll hear him when he knocks," I said quietly, so my panic and worry about Brad wouldn't echo between us.

"Yeah, I'll hear him if he knocks. Maybe I'll let him in."

I raised my eyebrows. "Maybe?"

He shrugged. "Thought he was rude, almost knocking his chair over in his hurry to be with the snow bunny."

I stared at him. "You didn't like her?"

He jerked his head back in revulsion at the thought and scrunched up his brow. "*Please.*"

I don't know why I took his response as an invitation, but I did. Maybe because it so reflected my opinion of "Cyn." It made us *compadres*, in sync, buddies. I lowered myself to the couch. "Why didn't you like her?"

"'I'm so sorry to bother you . . .'" He did a perfect imitation of her breathless delivery that made me want to laugh. "Give me a break," he said. "If she was really sorry, she wouldn't have walked over to begin with. A broken disposal isn't exactly an emergency."

I found it comforting that I wasn't the only one who was less than impressed with our neighbor, and I didn't think he was really expecting me to answer. I moved back into the corner of the couch and brought my feet up to the cushion. My legs weren't nearly as long as Joe's, so I couldn't stretch them out far enough to rest my feet on the coffee table.

"What are you watching?" I asked, deciding I could keep a lookout for Brad here as easily as I could from the deck.

"*Law and Order* rerun. I think they're on twenty-four–seven these days."

I snuggled down more deeply into the cushions. "I love *Law and Order*, except for the fact that there aren't nearly enough cute guys on the show."

"What are you talking about? Lennie was cute."

I could tell from his grin that he was teasing, but still I felt obligated to defend my position. "Too old. Still, it was sad when Jerry Orbach died."

"Yeah, I was sorry to hear that. I really liked the way he ended each intro with some wise-crack." He shook his head. "That Lennie."

"I was hoping when he left the show that

they'd replace him with some really young, sexy detective. I mean, it's not fair. Jack's assistants are young, sexy women."

"The show isn't about eye candy. It's got good writing. That's the real star of the show."

"So you'd be okay if the next time they replaced Jack's assistant, she wore orthopedic shoes, and her gray hair in a bun?"

"Hey, let's not get too carried away here. Don't need to eliminate the sweets completely . . . and maybe you have a point about not enough young guys."

I drew my legs closer to my body, wrapped my arms around them, and placed my chin on my knees. I liked the way that Joe never tried to bully me into anything, the way he'd helped keep things calm earlier when I'd presented my list of rules.

"Is that the reason Sam called you Mr. Law and Order? Because you like this show?"

"Nah, he calls me that because I'm majoring in criminal law."

"Are you going to be a lawyer?"

"No, I'm thinking more along the lines of

FBI, maybe CIA."

"Wow, that's pretty ambitious."

"Well, don't be too impressed. I still have three and a half years to go. A lot can happen between now and then. I gotta get all the basic coursework out of the way first."

I could see him working for the FBI or the CIA. He didn't have the overpowering presence that Brad did, but there was something about him that made me feel really safe, comfortable. He treated me like an equal, like someone whose opinion he valued, like I was interesting.

"Sam's never talked about you. How did you meet him?"

Not that Sam was in the habit of talking to me about his friends. As a matter of fact, he seldom talked to me about anything.

"We live in the same dorm. My room is across the hall from his."

"I didn't see you when I was there for family weekend."

"I know."

Something about the way he said it . . .

"Did you see me?" I asked.

"Yeah."

As though suddenly embarrassed, he looked at the TV, pointed at the screen. "Angie Harmon. My favorite."

It was strange. Sitting here in the dark with the dancing firelight and the flickering images from the TV washing over him, it occurred to me that he might be better looking than Brad. Not in the same rugged way that Brad was, of course. Brad was . . . well, Brad looked tough. Strong. Joe looked . . . well, he looked tough, too, but in a nicer kind of way. I wasn't making sense, couldn't sort out my thoughts.

But I discovered that I enjoyed watching him.

"What color are your eyes?" I asked.

He jerked his head around so fast that I thought I heard his neck pop.

"What?"

"Your eyes. I noticed them earlier, but I couldn't figure out what color they are."

I could make out his grin in the shadows.

"Depends on what I'm wearing. If it's blue, my eyes look blue. If I'm wearing green, they look green. Brown, brown." He rocked his head from side to side. "The official color on my driver's license is hazel."

I wasn't sure if I'd ever looked that closely at hazel eyes before. They were kind of intriguing. I was tempted to get up and turn on the light so I could get a better look at his, now that I knew what color they were, but it seemed like an odd thing to want to do.

"Your eyes are one clear-cut color," he said. "Green."

"You noticed, huh?"

He studied me for a heartbeat before turning his attention back to the show. "Yeah."

There it was again. Disappointment . . . or embarrassment.

But that made no sense. We were talking eye color for goodness' sake.

Joe wore his hair short on the sides and back, a little longer in the front. The strands had a mussed look, the way they might look if a girl had run her fingers through it. Brad's hair was cropped really short. I wouldn't be able to tell if the snow bunny next door had touched them. Thank goodness.

Joe had a well-defined jaw that sported a

day's growth of beard. I guess he would use my bathroom in the morning to shave. That sure seemed intimate. There was a bathroom downstairs between the two basement bedrooms, but the bathroom up here had a door that led into the living room and a door that led into my bedroom.

So, yeah, he'd probably be using my bathroom first thing. I needed to make sure I had the door leading into my bedroom closed.

I twisted around and looked at the front door. I heard Joe sigh like he was irritated with me or something.

"What if he tripped coming over here and he's out there freezing to death?" I asked. "I've heard that you don't know that you're dying because you start to get all warm and drowsy. You just think you're going to sleep."

"Trust me. He's not out there freezing to death. He didn't trip on his way back over here."

"How do you know?"

He gave me a sideways glance. "I just know."

Okay, so if he hadn't tripped . . . maybe there was another reason he hadn't come knocking on our door. But I so didn't want to think about that.

"He's probably staying over there, because he doesn't have a key and he didn't want to wake anyone up over here," I guessed.

"Yeah, I'm sure that's the reason."

But he said it like he was sure that *wasn't* the reason and he thought I was stupid for thinking it was, that I was stupid for not recognizing that Brad hadn't come home because Cynthia had given him a reason to stay over there. He wasn't so different from Sam. I guessed that was why they were friends. I suddenly didn't like him, his attitude, or his big bare feet resting on the coffee table. Why was I even here? I had skiing to do in the morning and I needed to be rested for it.

I popped up off the couch. "Well, I'm going to bed. Goodnight."

He looked at me, studying me again, like he was searching for something. "Don't let Sam get to you. It's a guy's job to torment his sisters."

I wasn't sure how we'd switched the topic from Brad to Sam, but I was okay with it. It was so much safer. It didn't involve my heart.

"It doesn't sound like you torment your sisters," I said.

"I *always* leave the toilet seat up."

"Then why did you agree to the rule?"

"Maybe I like you more than I like my sisters."

# Chapter 6

The next morning, while I took my shower, I tried really hard not to think about two things:

1. I never heard Brad come home.

2. Joe's parting words before I returned to bed.

And sometimes I found myself thinking harder and longer about Joe's words than about Brad's failure to return from next door. I was pretty sure that Joes's comment had been innocent with no innuendo, but then I'd think about the fact that he seemed embarrassed to have noticed me when I didn't notice him. Gosh, had he been in the dorm hallway? Had I looked right at him and not noticed him or remembered him?

Geez, what an insult to him if that was the

case. But he wasn't forgettable, so maybe he'd seen me from a distance—while I was walking with Sam and my parents across campus or something.

And he liked me more than he liked his sisters because that's just the way guys were. I mean, honestly, Sam liked Allie and Leah more than he liked me. He'd talked to them almost nonstop at the Pile It On, and he *never* talked to me that much.

So Joe's was a typical guy statement. It didn't mean anything.

I had myself convinced that's the way it was by the time I walked into the living room, dressed in jeans and a sweater. The drapes were drawn, so the room was in shadows.

I peered over at the couch. Joe was sprawled on it, a quilt draped over him, a pillow beneath his head, his bare feet hanging off one end. I resisted the urge to tug the quilt down and cover up those feet. They had to be cold, and he had to be uncomfortable. It didn't seem fair that he'd have to sleep there for three weeks. Maybe the guys would rotate sharing the beds.

But that was their problem. I wasn't giving

up my bed. Not even for a guy who liked me more than he liked his sisters.

I crept into the kitchen and turned on the light. I walked to the sink, reached over it, and opened the blinds. Through the window, I could see Cynthia's condo. I realized that I could have just come in here last night and kept an eye out instead of trying to get to the deck. Not that I still wouldn't have had to walk by Joe, but I could have made the excuse of needing a drink of water. Coming up with a reason for wanting to go out to the deck at midnight had proven a bit of a problem—not that I'd gotten far enough to make an excuse. Besides, Joe had pretty much guessed my intentions. I had a feeling that he wasn't quite as clueless as Sam.

I went to the refrigerator and took out a carton of eggs and a package of bacon. I would start cooking breakfast. I needed to focus on anything except the real reason that Brad hadn't returned—the very real possibility that he'd slept with Cynthia. So who was being clueless now?

I set everything on the counter and took a

couple of pans out of the cabinet. Brad wasn't my boyfriend, so he had the right to do whatever he wanted with whomever he wanted. But I didn't like the idea that he might have. And if he had, then should I give up on *us* completely?

Only there was no *us*, not really. So the question was, did I want an *us* with Brad if he had slept with "Cyn"?

"You broke the rules."

With a tiny screech, I spun around. Joe was lounging in the doorway, his shoulder pressed against the wall, his arms crossed over his chest, his biceps clearly visible. In the light of the kitchen I could read the T-shirt that I'd been unable to read the night before in the dark. It read, THESE GUNS DON'T COME WITH SAFETIES.

Ah, man! He had an amazing set of guns, which were also more visible in the light. He definitely worked out.

"What?" I snapped. If I'd said more than one word, I would have stammered. He had me totally rattled. Did Brad's arms look that strong? I crazily wondered what it might feel like to be held in Joe's arms, to look into those hazel eyes at close range.

"According to the rules, the guys are supposed to shower first," Joe said. "I wonder what punishment I should administer to you."

His gaze slowly roamed over me, stealing my breath as it went.

"Punishment?" I squeaked.

"It was decided yesterday that I would be the enforcer of the rules."

"Only for Sam."

"You sure?"

I nodded jerkily. "Besides, I didn't know anyone was already up."

And actually he hadn't been when I'd walked by.

"No big deal, Freckles."

"Why'd you call me that?"

"I don't know. Maybe because you remind me of Kate on *Lost*."

That was a major compliment. Kate was strong and confident, repeatedly kicking guys' butts. I hardly ever did that. I thought about telling him, but what the heck. Let him have his fantasy.

"Who's your favorite character on the show?" he asked.

I took a minute to respond to his change in direction.

"I liked Jack in the beginning, but Sawyer really grew on me."

"Yeah, I've always heard girls go for the bad boys. I guess that's the reason Brad has such a following."

I had a vision of Brad surrounded by maniacal, screaming women. I hoped Joe wasn't putting me in that category. It was insulting.

"What do you mean?" I asked.

"I mean wherever we go, girls are attracted to him. Like the snow bunny last night."

The reminder of our neighbor—and my failure to hold Brad's attention—hurt. "I didn't hear him come in."

"I'm not surprised."

"So he was really quiet when he came home?" I was pitiful. My voice sounded so hopeful and fearful at the same time. Like I was putting off facing the truth—Brad had done more than fix a stupid garbage disposal.

Joe just shook his head.

"Maybe he knocked—"

"I left the door unlocked."

As if on cue, I heard the front door open. My stomach tightened and my heart started pounding.

"Hey, Joe!" It was Brad. I'd recognize his voice anywhere and the way it shimmered through me. "Good news, man. Cyn is going to hang around with us on the slopes today."

His good news was my bad news.

Brad came around the corner, into the kitchen, and stopped short at the sight of me. I figured I probably looked the way our snowman would come summer: melting, melting, melting. Why couldn't he be as excited about me as he was about Cynthia?

He gave me a broad grin that for the span of a heartbeat offered me hope that maybe . . .

"Hey, Allie."

And the hope was gone, buried beneath an avalanche of disappointment. He was never going to get together with me. He didn't even remember my freaking name!

"She's Kate," Joe said quietly.

Brad shook a finger at me like I was the one

who got my name wrong. "That's right. Kate is the sister, Allie is the friend. Sam talked about them so much on the drive here, I got them confused. No big deal. I'm off to take a shower. I'll catch you guys later."

I stood there mute and devastated. Sam talked about me and Allie? Why would he do that? Why did I care? It was probably all bad. My brother must have turned him against me, revealing the most embarrassing moments of my childhood.

"Hey, Kate, don't let him get to you. He's not good with names." Joe's voice held pity and he was so wrong. Brad didn't have any trouble at all remembering Cyn.

I hated Joe at that moment. He knew, *knew* I liked Brad. I was wearing my heart on my sleeve. Something Aunt Sue always said, but I'd never really understood what it meant until now. It meant everyone — except stupid, dumb Brad — knew that I liked him.

I sprung into action and started to walk past Joe. He grabbed my arm. "Kate—"

"I have to go."

"Where are you going?"

"To Aunt Sue's for our morning meditation session."

He gave me a grin like he thought that was all I needed to make my world right again. "Thought the girls were supposed to cook breakfast."

I had to get out of there. Pronto. The last thing I wanted him to see were the tears burning the back of my eyes as they moved to the front and rolled over onto my cheeks. "Later."

I sounded like I was choking on those very tears. I broke away from his hold and grabbed my jacket from the coat rack by the door. I was stuffing my arms into the sleeves when I heard Sam announce, "Hey, Kate, I want my eggs over easy and my bacon crisp."

I hadn't seen him come into the living room, but I wasn't going to look back at him. He'd know something was wrong. Or maybe he wouldn't. Like I said, he was pretty clueless most of the time.

"Leave her alone, Sam," Joe said.

I was on the front porch, zipping my jacket, the door slammed shut behind me before Sam could say something else equally stupid. My brother was such an idiot.

Then I was running, running hard, down the hill, toward the village, toward Aunt Sue's, toward a haven away from the embarrassment I'd just suffered.

Joe knew what I felt for Brad. I'd seen it in his hazel eyes.

And he knew what Brad felt for me.

Absolutely nothing.

"Clear your mind and focus on your breathing, Katie," Aunt Sue said. "Release the negative energy."

I was sitting on an exercise mat on the carpeted floor in Aunt Sue's apartment, my back straight, my hands limp in my lap, my eyes closed.

In a panic I'd arrived at her apartment above the bookstore and pounded on her door. When she opened it, I'd rushed inside and burst into tears. Not so much because Brad had broken my heart. He hadn't. Not really. I mean, to break something you have to touch it, right? And he hadn't touched my heart yet.

I was simply majorly embarrassed that Joe

had witnessed my humiliation, and it had occurred to me during my mad dash over to Aunt Sue's that Sam might know what was going on as well. The last person, other than Joe, I wanted to know the affairs of my heart.

"Focus, Kate," Aunt Sue commanded in a soft, singsong voice. "Feel the air filling and expanding your lungs. Now, release . . . release . . . release . . ."

That was how meditation worked. You concentrated on your breathing, focused all your energy there—

"There's no place like home. There's no place like home. There's no place . . ." Aunt Sue's voice trailed off.

Once your focus was pinpointed on your breathing, you began running your own personal mantra through your head. Something that guided you, brought pleasant memories. Something that would take you to the next state of being. For Aunt Sue, it was *The Wizard of Oz*. Go figure.

That morning, mine was something that would bring me a great deal of satisfaction: Break a leg. Break a leg. Break a leg.

I was directing it toward Cynthia, which really isn't how meditation works. It's not like voodoo or something, where you try to throw a curse on someone, and, okay, it was a mean thought that I didn't really want to come true. And it wasn't exactly releasing negative energy. . . .

"I can't think of anything, Aunt Sue," I finally said.

"Then use mine."

Only I couldn't. I didn't want images of the good witch of the north who looked too much like Cynthia or a crazy wizard who could be my brother. Or perfect Dorothy holding perfect Toto. I bet Brad wouldn't have forgotten her name.

I opened my eyes and stretched out on the floor, inhaled the sweet fragrance of the candles burning around us. Aunt Sue didn't go with plain candle scents like vanilla or cinnamon. I was breathing in moonlight mist and secret garden and midnight passion.

I was breathing in a spicy and tangy scent. Brad.

No, it wasn't Brad. It was Joe. Last night

when we were sitting together on the couch. He didn't smell at all like Brad. Lemony was a better description. Lemony with his hair mussed and his feet bare. And the way he smiled whenever he looked at me. Not a big hey-am-I-a-stud-or-what smile like Brad gave me, but more of a I-like-looking-at-you smile. Like the smile was a gift to me or something. My presence was a gift to him.

Where did that thought come from?

"I see you finally relaxed," Aunt Sue said.

She had her arms lifted high over her head and was stretching at the waist from side to side. For a woman with gray hair, she was awfully limber.

"Not really. I was just thinking." I shrugged, which was a strange feeling with my back on the floor. "Nothing important."

"Everything's important."

I knew Aunt Sue dated. Over the years, she'd introduced me to several guys. They were always good-looking and fun. She never took her trips alone, but I never had a sense that she was totally serious about any of the guys.

"Why didn't you ever get married?" I asked.

"I almost did once," she said. A dreamy expression came over her face. "Loved him something fierce."

"So why didn't you marry him?"

"It just wasn't meant to be."

She rose to her feet, and I sat up. "You can't just leave it like that without giving me a real answer."

"Sure I can." She laughed and walked into the kitchen. A bar with stools separated it from the living room, so I could still see and hear her clearly. "Besides, the history of my love life isn't going to help you figure out yours. And isn't that the reason you're here this morning?"

"I'm here because we always meditate together," I lied.

"When you're staying with me, sure. But you're not going to traipse over here every morning, are you?"

Didn't anyone want me around?

"Would it bother you if I did?"

"Of course not. But I figured you'd want to spend time with your friends. Isn't that the reason you brought them?"

Without answering her, I got up and walked

over to the bar and sat on a stool. I watched as Aunt Sue prepared her morning shake. She put all kinds of healthy stuff in it. Whey protein, fruit . . .

"I thought I'd help you in the bookstore today."

She turned away from the blender and gave me a pointed stare. "That's what you thought, huh?"

"Yeah." I scrunched up my face. I knew what her expression meant. Honesty time. "I don't want to see Brad with Cynthia."

"So you're going to hide away?"

"Just today."

"Mmm-uh," she said, like she could see through my lie, and knew I was considering never again returning to the slopes. "I think you're making a big mistake, but it's your life."

She pushed the button on the blender, the buzzing stopping us from talking further. Which was fine by me.

I didn't have anything else to say, anyway.

# Chapter 7

*A*llie and Leah were totally bummed when I called to tell them that Aunt Sue needed help in her shop, so I was going to forego skiing. I tried to make it sound like I was making some great sacrifice for Aunt Sue, instead of what was really going on. I simply couldn't stand the thought of seeing Brad with Cynthia, or Joe looking at me like he thought I was a total loser for not hiding my feelings any better than I did.

"But what about Operation Hook-Brad-Up-With-Kate?" Leah asked.

"Please tell me that you're in your bedroom where the guys can't hear you." Using my cell phone, I'd called *her* cell phone, so as far as I knew, she was sitting at the breakfast table surrounded by everyone.

"I'm outside making a snow girl for our snowman. He was getting lonely. Allie's helping me."

"And the guys?"

"Following the rules, cleaning the kitchen. You missed a scrumptious breakfast. Did you know Allie knows how to make omelets? The guys were majorly impressed."

So was I. "I had no idea. I had breakfast with Aunt Sue." The energy shake. An omelet sure sounded good, though.

"Okay, great, we won't worry about you eating, but what about Operation—"

"Not today, Leah. Aunt Sue really needs me to help her, and I figure it's the least I can do since she's letting us use the condo." I looked behind me to make sure my jeans hadn't caught on fire yet from all the lying.

"Well, we should help, too, then."

"No, she just needs one person. Not too much room behind the counter. We'd just get in each other's way."

"Are you sure? I feel guilty going to the slopes without you. Allie's nodding. She feels guilty, too."

"Look, I've skied before, so I don't need lessons. Y'all take the class today and learn the basics. Tomorrow we'll be able to ski on the slopes together."

"I guess you're right. Besides, you don't need to hook up with a ski instructor, since Brad is here. As for me, I may need more than one day of lessons."

"You won't. It just takes a few hours to learn the basics. Trust me."

"We'll see. Oops! Sam just came out on the deck to give us the we're-leaving-right-now signal, so we've gotta run. But I promise Allie and I will stop by the shop this afternoon for some hot chocolate, after we leave the slopes."

"Sounds like a plan. Y'all have fun."

I closed my cell phone and took a deep breath. I figured a day to regain my equilibrium was all I needed. A day to completely sever my one-sided bond with Brad. Tomorrow I would definitely go to the slopes, and I'd find that stud of a ski instructor. Lessons or no, I'd find him.

Unlike Leah and Allie, who were planning to grab hot chocolate *after* a day of skiing, a lot of people wanted the hot chocolate swirling through their system before they headed for the slopes. So for a while that morning, it was a madhouse, and I was rethinking my plan to avoid the guys.

My feet started to ache as I worked behind the counter, mixing one mug of hot chocolate after another. Fifty varieties arranged in alphabetical order. Most I never touched. Plain old chocolate, dark chocolate, or white chocolate were the most requested. And of course, I periodically fixed myself some mint chocolate, my absolute favorite.

Once things slowed down, I browsed through the bookstore looking for a good read. I always found some sort of treasure whenever I looked through the shelves. Aunt Sue was a voracious reader, so she and I always spent a lot of time over our winter breaks reading and discussing books. Or at least we had in the past. With Allie and Leah here, not to mention Sam and his friends, I didn't know how much time I'd have for actual reading. Especially if I did find a ski instructor.

"We just got in a new one from the Fingerprints series," Paige said.

I looked over my shoulder at Aunt Sue's assistant manager, Paige Turner. She swore that was her real name, but I didn't believe her. I mean honestly, what were the odds of someone with a name like that working in a bookstore?

"Thanks." I took the paperback book she was offering me.

"I think Sue lives for these winter breaks when you come to see her," Paige said. She had blonde hair that reminded me of Cynthia's, but her attitude was so different. Plus she talked and breathed like a normal person. I couldn't help but like Paige. She wasn't that much older than me, having gone straight from high school to the bookstore a few years back. Or at least that was her story. I had another theory on how she'd ended up here.

"I'm sure someone who has scaled Mount Everest lives for spending time with me," I said, smiling.

"Hey, she really does. You're her favorite niece."

I laughed. "I'm her *only* niece."

"Well, then, aren't you special?"

I felt my smile grow. It was one of the reasons I loved being there: I always ended up feeling good about myself. "Why, yes, I am."

"So why are you hanging around here instead of on the slopes with a cute ski instructor?"

"What is it with everyone trying to set me up with a ski instructor?" I asked.

Her blue eyes widened. "I didn't know everyone was."

"Pretty much, yeah."

"I guess because they're usually a lot of fun. Some of us are getting together at the lodge tonight. You and your friends should join us. I'll even take the time to point out the available instructors to you."

"Thanks. I'll let my friends know."

"Be sure you bring that cutie who was with your brother yesterday."

"Hate to disappoint you, but I think he's already hooked up with someone permanently."

"Bummer! That happened fast."

"Yeah." It sure did.

She shook her head in wonder. "She who

hesitates, I guess. I should have made my move yesterday."

Great. She liked Brad, too. Still, I couldn't dislike her because of it. She wasn't at all like Cynthia. If I told her I had interest in a guy, she'd back off. I didn't think Cynthia knew the meaning of the phrase.

"What about Sam's other friend? The one with the dark hair?" Paige asked.

I stared at her, trying to decipher her meaning. "Wait a minute. When you said to bring the cutie . . . weren't you talking about the one with the dark hair?"

"Heck, no. I was talking about the blond. What was his name? Jim? Jack?"

"Joe."

She flashed a smile that would do a game-show hostess proud. "Right. Joe. Is he the one who's no longer available?"

"Uh, no. Brad is the one."

"Well, that's great!" She wiggled her brows and patted my shoulder. "Be sure and bring Joe. We'll swap: friend for ski instructor."

That sounded fair. Even though I didn't know how Joe might feel about it. Still, I found myself nodding. "Okay."

"I can't wait!" Paige said.

"Me, either."

Paige went back to placing the new shipment of books on the shelves. So she preferred Joe over Brad.

Wasn't that interesting? It looked like all the guys were going to end up matched with someone. Well, all except for Sam. I truly couldn't imagine anyone wanting to purposely hook up with my irritating brother.

By mid-afternoon, I was almost ready to admit that Aunt Sue had been right. Working in the shop wasn't nearly as much fun as playing on the slopes. Mainly because once everyone had their morning hot chocolate fix, they were off to the mountains, leaving me curled up on one of the love seats in front of the fireplace, toasting my toes while periodically looking up from the book I was reading to stare at the snow-covered mountains and wondering what was happening on them.

Had Allie and Leah finished their ski lessons? Had they flirted with an instructor? Had

Cynthia broken a leg? Had Brad? Either scenario might be satisfying.

Or I could simply not care. Could stop thinking about them. Why invest my energy in even wondering what Brad was doing? He didn't know who I was. So I'd just forget who he was.

It sounded like a plan. I spent my afternoon retreat working on not thinking about Brad. Not caring. Envisioning the satisfaction I'd feel when I deleted his picture from my computer's wallpaper list.

By late afternoon, I was totally over him. It wasn't going to bother me to see him with Cynthia. I'd moved beyond him.

Looking out the window, I saw a group of people trudging up the boardwalk, bundled in ski jackets, and I figured they were going to be stopping by for some hot chocolate. We usually had an afternoon rush as people began leaving the slopes, heading home for the day. I set aside my book and went behind the counter to await their arrival.

And I found myself wishing that I'd looked at them a little more closely as they'd approached.

Then I would have realized that sneaking out the back door was the way to go, because when they came inside, laughing and happy, Brad's arm slung around Cynthia, I realized that I hadn't gotten over Brad.

I wasn't even close to getting over him.

# Chapter 8

" Hey, Kate, we missed you," Leah said, as she sat on a stool at the counter.

"We were so busy today, I hardly had time to think. I don't know what Aunt Sue would have done if I hadn't been here to help out. It was chaos." I was babbling. "What can I get you guys?" Another lie, maybe?

Everyone lined up on the stools at the counter: Cynthia, Brad, Sam, Allie, Leah, Joe.

I really felt like the odd one out, standing on the other side. My own fault entirely. Avoidance. You can't be part of the crowd if you're not *with* the crowd.

Cynthia ordered Guilty Pleasure—why was I not surprised? Everyone else just wanted plain old hot chocolate with mini-marshmallows sprinkled on top. I decided to fix myself another mug of mint chocolate, just so I would feel like I was part of the group.

"Hey, gang, how'd it go?" Aunt Sue asked as she stepped out of her back office. She spent a good deal of time in there working up her supply orders and going over spreadsheets on her computer.

Everyone started talking at once.

"Awesome!" Allie.

"The cutest ski instructor." Leah.

"Went down Devil's Peak." Sam.

"Such fun!" Cynthia.

"He was so incredibly hot." Leah again about the ski instructor.

"What a rush!" Brad.

But I didn't think he was referring to the ski instructor. Like I said, everyone was talking at once.

Aunt Sue was laughing. Joe wasn't saying anything, just sipping on his hot chocolate, watching me, like he was patiently waiting for the moment when I reached across the counter, wrapped my hands around Cynthia's throat, and strangled her.

"I have some good news to share," I said when the exclamations died down. "Paige invited us to a party at the lodge tonight."

My announcement received another set of exclamations.

"Awesome!"

"What's the lodge?"

"A hangout."

"Totally cool!"

"Oh, gosh, I absolutely adore parties. I need to get home so I can start getting ready." Cynthia's announcement caused silence to fall as she slid off the stool.

"I'll go with you," Brad said.

Could he get any more pathetic? I watched him traipse out the door after her like a dog trailing after a bone.

"You managed to beat the crowd," Aunt Sue told the others. She laid a hand on my shoulder. "Why don't you take a break before it gets really busy in here? I'm sure you have a lot to catch up on."

"Sounds good to me."

I directed the others to grab their mugs and join me near the fire. Only Allie and Leah took me up on the offer, which was cool. I was only being polite when I invited the remaining guys. I didn't really want them there, because I knew Allie and Leah wouldn't tell me as much if we had an audience. So it was okay by me that they stayed at the counter and talked with Aunt Sue.

"How was it really?" I asked after we sat down.

"Totally awesome," Allie said. "I thought my heart was going to stop when I watched Sam go down Devil's Peak. But he is such a great skier. Not at all afraid."

Devil's Peak was one of the trails designated for the more advanced skiers. The trail started above the tree line. The tree line marks the spot where the altitude is so high that trees don't grow there. It's great for skiing. The Devil's Peak trail eventually narrows down once it reaches the tree line, but until then, skiers have room to maneuver and an unobstructed view.

"You watched him?" I asked, surprised anyone would want to. I mean, this was my brother we were talking about here. Not some hottie hunk.

"I ended up there because we went on the

ski lift together. I'd never been on a ski lift before so he offered to show me how it works. My heart was pounding so hard when I realized that the lift kept moving and that we were supposed to get off it by skiing. I don't think I could have done it if he hadn't held my arm. After he skied down the slope, he took the lift back up and we rode it down together."

"Sounds like a regular Prince Charming."

"He was," she said, her cheeks turning red. "And I liked watching him ski. He's really good. I was impressed. I'll never be able to ski down a trail like that."

"Sure you will," I said.

"Today I didn't actually ski on anything other than the bunny slope, but at least I graduated from ski class." She jerked her thumb at Leah. "Klutz over here has to take the class again tomorrow."

Leah wiggled her eyebrows, not at all offended. "You bet. Ian is such a hottie. He's Australian and has the most delicious accent. I adore it. He promised to give me private lessons if I don't do any better tomorrow." She leaned forward and whispered, "I won't do any better tomorrow."

"He's that hot, huh?"

"His presence melts snow."

I laughed. "I've got to see this guy."

"Just remember that I had first dibs on him."

I watched the marshmallows bobbing in my hot chocolate. "I guess Brad hung around with Cynthia all day."

"Like a sliver of metal against a magnet."

I grimaced. "She's too old for him. She's gotta be like, I don't know, twenty-four."

"At least," Leah said.

I wondered what Brad really saw in her, other than her tight pants and too-small sweaters.

"Whenever she talks, she sounds like she's on the verge of hyperventilating," Allie said.

I laughed. "She does take heavy breathing to the extreme."

"You wouldn't have liked seeing the way she sat on Brad's lap in your brother's SUV, 'practicing' for tomorrow when you'd be with us and there wouldn't be enough seats."

"Great," I mumbled.

My parents had given Sam the SUV when

he'd graduated from high school. It gave him freedom that I didn't yet have. He and his buds had been able to drive up while my friends and I had flown.

Of course, we'd left from different destinations as well. Allie, Leah, and me from home, the guys from college. The university was about six hours from where we lived, so I completely understood Sam not wanting to come and get me, even if he had known I'd be there. Besides, I wouldn't have wanted to be in a vehicle with him for fifteen hours, anyway. Fifteen minutes with him was a stretch of my patience.

"I think I'm just going to have to give up on Brad," I muttered.

"Maybe not," Leah said. "What's Cynthia got that you don't?"

"Lots of curves." I wasn't totally flat, but my chest resembled hills, while Cynthia's looked more like the Grand Tetons. And my hips didn't exactly flare out, not that I wanted them to.

"Look, we're going to that party tonight," Leah said. "We'll all look our best, and before the night is over, maybe Brad will come around to noticing that you have a lot more to offer personality-wise than Cynthia. And you don't have any trouble talking and breathing at the same time."

"I doubt he'll notice me."

"Don't be such a negative Nancy," Leah said.

I rolled my eyes. "Have you been talking to Aunt Sue?" Aunt Sue had all kinds of quaint descriptions: Sad Sally, Happy Hannah.

Leah grinned. "Come on. So Brad spent the day with Cynthia—"

"Let's not forget that he also spent the night with her."

"Probably because he didn't have a key and a way to get in. Give him a reason to want to be with you tonight."

I nodded. "Okay."

But I was also wondering if I wanted him that badly. Was he really worth it?

"Hey, you girls walking, or riding back to the condo with me?" Sam asked.

Allie popped off the loveseat. "Riding."

Leah got up, too. "How long are you gonna work?"

"I'll help with the late afternoon rush, then I'll be back at the condo."

"Okay, we'll see you later."

I sipped on my hot chocolate, contemplating what I might wear for the party. Most of my sweaters were bulky, designed to keep me warm rather than to show off the shape of my body. I thought about stopping by the Knitted Cable to see if I could find something that might prove a little more interesting to Brad. It was a boutique. All the stores in the village were labeled a shop or a boutique—they weren't really big enough to be anything else. And they all smelled like pine and were as cozy as a fire in winter. I guess because most had fireplaces and it was winter.

I heard a footstep and turned my head to see Joe standing there. I hadn't realized he was still hanging around. I should have. I mean, I hadn't seen him leave, but he just wasn't on my radar. Not totally true. He was on my radar, I just preferred that he not be. After all, he'd witnessed one of my more humiliating moments.

He held up a paper bag that looked like it contained a book. "I was browsing. Looks like I got left behind."

"Yeah, Sam already left with Leah and Allie."

"That's all right. What's a little walk after

trudging up mountains all day?" He sat down on the loveseat across from mine. "Think you'll go with us tomorrow?"

"Probably. How did you enjoy the lessons?"

"Didn't take any. I know how to ski."

I felt myself blush. "I'm sorry. I didn't know."

"No reason you would know."

"So you're not as mesmerized by all this as Allie and Leah are? No building snowmen for you?"

"Sure, I build snowmen, and make snow angels. It's the magic of snow. It's gotta be done."

"You don't agree with Sam that playing in snow is just for kids?"

"The way I play in snow isn't for kids. Maybe I'll show you sometime."

Those hazel eyes of his unexpectedly darkened, and I thought maybe he was thinking about things that would warm up a girl. Dangerous things.

Now where did that thought come from? Brad was the danger, not Joe. Or at least I didn't think the danger was Joe. But the way my heart was thudding against my chest, I suddenly wasn't so sure.

"Have you ever been to Snow Angel Valley before?" I asked, wanting to change the subject.

"No, but I'll be sure to come back. It's beautiful country. I love being around mountains. I grew up on the Texas coast—flat as a pancake."

I hadn't known that, either, but then we really hadn't talked except for last night while I was making my pitiful attempt not to look like I was waiting for Brad. And we hadn't delved into each other's histories.

"Where did you learn to ski?"

"Wyoming, New Mexico, other parts of Colorado. My folks would take us every year." He shook his head from side to side as though contemplating how much to tell me, how much I might really be interested. He gave a little nod like he'd made his decision. "I prefer rock climbing and mountain climbing, though."

"You and Aunt Sue should talk. She scaled Everest."

"We did talk. She's a fascinating lady."

"She's definitely that."

"Do you have any interest in mountain climbing?"

"I like to hike snowy trails through the mountains, but it's not the same thing."

"No, it's not. When we were walking through town, I noticed that a little theater is showing *Touching the Void*. Have you seen it?"

I remembered hearing something about the movie. The Last Buck Theater—which did, in fact, have a stuffed deer standing outside the entrance and only charged a dollar—usually showed movies that had already done their time on prime cable channels. The more obscure the movie, the more likely it would make an appearance at the Last Buck.

"Wasn't that a documentary about those two English guys who almost died on a mountain?" I asked.

"Yeah, one had to cut the other guy's rope when he was dangling over a crevasse. It's really incredible that either of them survived." He hesitated. "Don't suppose you'd want to go see it?"

"What? The movie?"

"Yeah."

"Sure. Why not? Maybe tomorrow night, since we have the party tonight. I'll check with Allie and Leah and see if they're up for it."

He pressed his lips together into this funny shape like he was trying to stop himself from saying something.

"Right," he finally said. "Yeah, let's see if everyone wants to go."

Oh, gosh, sometimes I'm as clueless as my brother.

"You weren't asking me out on a date, were you?"

"Heck, no. I just wanted to see the movie and thought it might be fun to not see it alone. The more the merrier." He stood and tapped the bag against his leg. "So I guess—"

Whatever he was going to say was lost as a crowd of people came through the door. Snow Angel Valley's version of the rush hour traffic had just descended upon us.

# Chapter 9

$\mathcal{J}$oe surprised the heck out of me by not heading out the door as soon as it was clear of customers stampeding inside. Instead he shucked off his ski jacket, hung it on the coat rack in the corner, shoved up the sleeves on his sweatshirt, revealing those amazing forearms, and said, "Tell me what to do."

The task that required the least amount of instruction was taking orders, so I gave him a pad of paper and a pencil and set him off to find out what kind of brew the people wanted. Aunt Sue and Paige joined us.

I was mixing chocolate with warm milk — Aunt Sue's *secret* ingredient. Real whole milk, which was a total surprise coming from someone who thought nothing of tossing freshly squeezed asparagus juice into her morning shake. I'd have thought she'd go with skim milk, but nope — whole all the way. And she definitely doesn't believe in using those hot chocolate mixes that require water.

"Hot chocolate should be sinful, and I don't believe in sinning in half measures." Her words, not mine.

So I stood at the back of the counter adding two scoops of chocolate powder and eight ounces of whole milk — warmed on a burner, not in a microwave. I stirred until the powder was dissolved — hand-stirring was another secret — dropped in mini-marshmallows, and set the mug on the proper tile that identified the type of hot chocolate inside. A section of the back counter was comprised of rows of blue tiles, etched with the name of the chocolate that went there. Aunt Sue had efficiency down to an art form.

Joe grabbed the mugs and took them to the appropriate customers. Clockwork. We were in complete sync. I was amazed.

During one brief lull, he leaned over to me and whispered, "I meant to ask you earlier.

Paige Turner? That can't be her real name."

I peered over my shoulder at Paige before looking back at Joe and shaking my head. "No. My theory is that she's in the witness protection program. Maybe she got to pick her own name and said, 'I want to be Paige Turner working in a bookstore at a small ski resort.'"

Joe chuckled. "I guess that's a better explanation than having parents with a wicked sense of humor."

"It's only wicked if they'd known she was going to work in a bookstore."

"Good point." He grabbed the mug of Delightful Decadence and walked away. No, it wasn't exactly a walk. It was more of a swagger, brimming with confidence.

And confident was surely what he was. He'd never worked here before, but the customers couldn't tell from looking at him. He smiled and chatted and took their orders as though he'd been doing it all his life.

I was impressed. He was really quite charming, and I thought his ability to fit in would probably serve him well if he did ever go to work for the FBI or the CIA. Watch out, bad guys. Joe would have their number, charming them into confessing their illegal activities.

Twilight had arrived by the time the crowd diminished enough so that Joe and I could leave.

"Don't forget about the party," Paige called out as Joe and I were walking out the door.

I waved back at her. "We won't. See you soon."

"Both of you!"

I looked back at her and gave her a thumbs-up sign. When Joe and I were on the sidewalk, walking up the hill toward the condo, I said, "Paige has the hots for you."

Joe stopped walking. I stopped as well and looked at him.

"You're kidding."

I shook my head and smiled. "Nope. She told me."

I wasn't sure if he was blushing or if it was the cold breeze chapping his cheeks.

"Maybe I'll skip the party."

"Why?"

"You think I want to get involved with some-one in the witness protection program?"

I laughed. "That's just my theory. Besides, if you get close to her, maybe you can learn the truth about her name."

"What's it worth to you?"

I stared at him. "What are you talking about?"

"For me to go undercover, to get the information you want."

I rolled my eyes and gave him an impatient look. "Don't do it for me. Do it for yourself, because you're interested in her."

"Only I'm not. So I guess we'll never learn the truth about her past."

He started walking again and I fell into step beside him.

"How can you not be interested in her?"

"How can you be interested in Brad?"

Okay. I wasn't expecting that. Now *I* was the one to stop walking, my heart pounding hard enough to start an avalanche. Joe stopped as well, turned slowly, an eyebrow raised as though he actually expected me to answer his nosy question. I won't even go into why his question was nosy and mine wasn't, but it had something to do with my heart being involved and his not.

"My interests are none of your business," I finally managed through the lump of emotion that had settled in my throat.

"And my lack of interest in Paige is none of yours."

"You don't have to get so touchy. I wasn't trying to butt into your business. I just thought you might want to know that someone thinks you're hot."

"Well, I don't need you doing any match-making for me. I happen to be very interested in someone else around here."

"Then you should have asked her to the movie."

"I did."

"And she said no?"

Sighing, he shook his head. "Forget it."

He started trudging up the hill again.

I hurried after him. "Did you meet her on the slopes?"

"None of your business."

"Does Sam know about her?"

"None of your business."

"If you point her out to me tomorrow, I'll put in a good word for you."

"I don't need you putting in a good word for me."

He was walking so fast that I was having a difficult time keeping up. He really was in good shape. He had to do aerobic workouts in addition to the weights or whatever it was he did to keep those firm muscles.

"Oh, wait, maybe she'll be at the party tonight," I said. Wouldn't that be interesting? I wondered if I needed to warn Paige so she wouldn't get her heart broken.

"She will be," Joe said.

"How do you know?"

"I just know."

"You sure 'just know' a lot of stuff."

"Yep."

"Maybe you can make a move on her at the party."

"I doubt it."

"Why?"

"She's not interested in me."

"How can she not be interested?"

He spun around. I came up short, almost barreling into him.

"You tell me," he demanded.

"Tell you what?"

"How she cannot be interested? Or better yet, why *would* she be interested?"

"You're nice."

He grimaced. "So is my grandmother."

"You're hardly a grandmother. Dress up tonight. That's what I'm doing. Then pour on the charm."

"That's your plan for the night? To pour on the charm?"

I heaved a sigh. "I'm going to try." Make a last ditch effort to win Brad over.

Joe slowly shook his head. "You don't have to try, Kate. Or dress up. You're terrific just the way you are."

I couldn't believe I was going to say this, but it wasn't as though I was revealing anything he didn't already know. "Then why doesn't Brad notice me?"

"He's an idiot."

I barked out a bit of laughter. "So is the girl you met on the slopes."

"I didn't say I met her on the slopes."

"Then where did you meet her?"

"How come I can't get it through your head—

none of your business!" He reached down, grabbed a handful of snow, and tossed it at me.

"Hey!"

I rushed past him. Felt snow hit my back. Without stopping, I reached down and scooped up my own handful, packed it together as I ran into the front yard of the condo, then spun around—

And went flying as Joe tackled me to the snow-laden ground. When I tried to gather up snow to toss at him, he grabbed my wrists and held them in place beside my head. He was heavy on top of me, straddling me, but it didn't hurt.

His face was so close to mine that I got a real good look at the color hazel. I was intrigued—by the color and the way he was studying me.

"Don't try to hook me up with anyone, Kate," he finally said.

I nodded slowly, my breath not having found me yet. "Okay."

We stayed there, just staring at each other. I was barely aware of the cold beneath me, because I was so aware of the guy on top of me.

"Are you going to let me up?" I eventually asked.

"Is there going to be dancing at that party tonight?"

Where did that question come from? I shrugged as much as I was able. "I don't know."

"Will you dance with me if there is?"

"Sure."

He grinned. "Then I'll let you up."

But he just stayed there, smiling and looking at me, until he finally shook his head and muttered, "Brad really is an idiot."

Then he rolled off me, got to his feet, and pulled me to mine. As we walked up the steps to the condo, I couldn't help wondering if maybe I was an idiot as well.

# Chapter 10

"*H*ot dogs?" Sam asked. "That's your idea of cooking a meal? Hot dogs?"

We were sitting at the dining room table. I glowered at Sam. "We're short on time because we have a party to get ready for. Besides, there's bound to be food there. Consider this a snack."

"I love hot dogs," Brad said. He'd come back from Cynthia's shortly after we got home.

"Clean-up should be a breeze," Joe said.

"Absolutely." I smiled at Sam. "So there."

"What are we going to have tomorrow?"

"We were thinking stew," Allie said.

Sam looked over at her, and I thought she was actually blushing.

"We could put all the ingredients in the crock pot before we leave in the morning, and they'd simmer all day. If you like stew," she said.

"Yeah, I like stew," he said.

"Since when?" I asked.

He glared at me. "It's got meat and potatoes in it, doesn't it?"

"And vegetables."

"I can pick them out."

"We don't have to put vegetables in there," Allie said.

"Yeah, we do," I said. "Otherwise, it'll be boring."

"Maybe we should take a vote," she said.

"I don't think we want our menus determined by a committee."

"Kate's right," Leah said. "There's always going to be something that someone doesn't like."

Allie shrugged. "I just wanted to be fair."

"Whatever y'all cook will be fine," Sam said, looking at Allie again.

Whoa! Was this my brother talking?

He looked over at me. "Except for hot dogs."

"Whatever. Like I said, we were short on time."

"Just make sure you fix a lot of whatever it

is, because we'll be hungry after skiing all day."

"We'll take care of it, Sam."

"Speaking of taking care of things, your aunt sure is taking good care of us," Leah said. "The pantry, the freezer, they're full of food. I don't think we'll have to do much shopping while we're here."

"She likes taking care of us," I told her.

"She's always been like that," Sam confirmed. "I think because the first time Mom and Dad left us here, Kate cried the entire time."

"I didn't cry the *entire* time," I said. "Besides, I was six."

"Remember the year we sneaked down to the store after she'd gone to sleep and ate all the marshmallows?"

Nodding, I laughed. "I was what? Eight?"

"Yeah. I've never been so sick in my life."

"I couldn't stand the sight of a marshmallow for the longest time," I admitted.

"Good times," Sam said. "We've had lots of good times here. And more to come, starting tonight."

I shoved back my chair, stood, and grinned at him. "Not until after you clean up."

❖ ❖ ❖

"What do you think?" I asked. "Is this too much?"

Allie, Leah, and I were all in my bedroom getting ready for the party. We'd decided that was the best way to do it. We'd hog one bathroom and let the guys get ready downstairs.

Leah smiled. "You look great!"

I was wearing a green cowl-necked sweater. The sleeves hugged my arms and went down to my knuckles. I loved the way they covered my hands, leaving only my fingers visible. The sweater itself wasn't too bulky, so my figure wasn't hidden away. I was wearing jeans. It was absolutely too cold to wear a skirt. There wasn't a lot of parking in the heart of the village, so it was impossible to know how far we might have to walk.

Leah and Allie agreed with my assessment of wearing a skirt. They were in jeans, too. And sweaters. Leah wore a red turtleneck sweater, and Allie wore a pink one with fluffy white fur at the collar. Leah with her short, dark hair looked mysterious; Allie with her blonde hair draped around her shoulders looked delicate.

I was somewhere in the middle, not too mysterious, not too delicate. The three of us could be a bedtime story.

I'd applied a hot iron to my hair to try to straighten out some of the natural curl. And I'd used some light green shadow to highlight my eyes.

"I don't look like I'm trolling for guys, do I?" I asked, a little unsure about the makeup, worried that it was a bit too much.

"You mean like Cynthia next door?"

I grimaced. "Yeah."

"You gotta fight fire with fire," Leah said.

"So I look like a skank?"

"No," my friends both assured me at the same time.

"You look like you want guys to notice you," Leah said. "But we all do, right? That's the whole point of going to a party. To hook up with guys."

"Right."

"And tonight is all about getting you with Brad."

I stared at my reflection in the mirror. Was it?

"Right?" Allie asked, as though reading my mind.

"Right."

"So what's up with you and Joe?" she asked.

"Why would you think there was anything?" I picked up my brush and started dragging it through my hair. It created static electricity, causing the strands to start flying around my head like Medusa's snakes. I should have left well enough alone.

"Maybe the fact that you came in with him before supper and you were both laughing and breathless."

"Laughing leaves you breathless."

"Your cheeks were flushed."

"They were cold. Besides, I told you. He stayed and helped during the rush at the hot chocolate counter."

"I think he likes you," Allie said.

"He likes someone, but I don't think it's me. He kinda mentioned her today." I spun around. "Speaking of kinda liking someone, this morning Aunt Sue told me that she was once in love."

Leah and Allie smiled as though I'd shared the secret of the century, their eyes huge. "Really? Who is he?"

"I don't know. She wouldn't say. She thought

she was going to marry him."

"What happened?" Allie asked.

"I don't know. Like I said. She wouldn't say. She was her usual mysterious self."

"I'll bet there's a picture of him hanging somewhere in her store."

I stared at Allie. I hadn't thought of that. A lot of the photos did have guys in them. "I'll bet you're right. I've looked at all of them, but not that closely."

"Tomorrow we'll have to go on a hunt through the shop, study all the photos, and see if we can figure out who he was," Leah said.

"I'll bet he was hot," Allie said. "He had to be hot."

"Maybe he was an artic explorer," Leah said.

"In which case he'd be cold," I said.

"Lame, Kate!" Leah shouted.

We were still laughing when we stepped into the living room, ready to go.

And came up short.

Had my stupid brother actually styled his dark hair? And what was this? A button-up shirt? Guess he was hoping to hook up with someone at the party as well. Whoever he ended up with would have my deepest sympathy.

"What's that stink?" I asked.

"It's some fancy aftershave," Sam said, jerking his head to the side.

That's when I noticed Joe standing there, grimacing. I grimaced, too. I thought I'd been insulting Sam. Apparently another miscalculation on my part.

"Moves, by Adidas," Joe mumbled.

"And we're all planning to make some moves tonight," Sam said. "Let's go."

"What about Brad?" I asked.

"He already went to get Cyn. They'll meet us there."

I did my best to hide my disappointment, but since Brad had joined us for supper, I'd mistakenly thought he was back over playing with us. Why didn't he just move next door already?

We all grabbed our jackets and stuffed our bodies into them while heading to the door.

"Are you driving?" I asked Sam.

"Nope. I plan to do some drinking," Sam said.

"You're not old enough," I reminded him.

"Never stopped me before."

"Sam!"

He halted and glared at me. "What? You gonna tattle to Mom and Dad?"

Was I? No. But he didn't know that. Besides, as irritating as my brother was, he was good for one thing: blackmail. And it was payback time for the snowball he'd hit me with yesterday.

"Not if you make a contribution to the Kate-have-a-good-time fund."

"Ah, Kate, come on. I'm not hurting anyone. I'm a responsible drinker."

"How can you be responsible if you're breaking the law?"

"I don't drive when I drink. No one gets hurt except me, if I happen to fall flat on my face."

"You get that drunk?"

"I've got better things to do than discuss my life with you." He reached into his back pocket and pulled out his wallet. "How much?"

"Twenty should do it."

"Five."

"Ten."

He held out the bill that had one of my favorite presidents on it. "You know, Kate, no one likes a snitch."

I snatched it from his fingers, folded it up, and shoved it into the front pocket of my jeans. "Payback's a bitch, Brother."

"What?"

"I wouldn't have tattled. But I didn't like getting hit with a snowball yesterday, either. So now we're even."

He snapped his fingers. "Give it back."

"Nope. Possession is nine-tenths of the law."

"You don't even know what that means."

"And I suppose you do."

"Hey, y'all, can we go?" Leah asked. "The cute guys are gonna be taken by the time we get there."

"No, they won't be," Sam said. "Because you'll be arriving with them."

I rolled my eyes. "Please, give us a break!"

Sam jerked open the door. "Let's go."

We all filed past. He closed and locked the door, and we were on our way. Somehow Sam took the lead with Allie and Leah flanking him, leaving me and Joe trudging along behind them.

I glanced over at Joe. He was wearing a turtleneck sweater and a leather jacket. He didn't even have the jacket buttoned up. His hands were shoved in the front pockets of his jeans, and he was staring at the sidewalk like he expected it to disappear at any second and he wanted to be prepared. I think he'd styled his hair, too.

"Aren't you cold?" I asked.

"Nope."

Eyes straight ahead. Jaw clenched. I didn't think the tight muscles in his jaw were because of the cold. Although I could have been wrong.

"Your aftershave doesn't stink. I thought Sam was wearing it. I was just giving him a hard time. It actually smells good."

He smelled really good, as a matter of fact.

He sliced his gaze over to me. If I'd been a snowman, the heat in his eyes would have turned me into a puddle of melted snow.

"The bottle slipped and splashed too much on me. I didn't want to take time for another shower. If I'd known you and Sam were going to go at it for so long, I would have taken the time."

"Don't you and your sisters ever pester each other?"

"Sure, but you and Sam are at it constantly.

You should cut the guy some slack."

"That works two ways you know."

"Yeah, I know. Your brother's not such a bad guy."

"You're just saying that because you're his friend."

"I guess. So since I tossed snow at you earlier, am I going to have to make a contribution to the Kate-have-a-good-time fund?" he asked.

I angled my chin haughtily. "You might. It'll cost you more, though, since you also tackled me to the ground."

"I'm strapped for cash. We might have to work it out in trade."

"What kind of trade?"

He gave me a grin that made me think I was in deep trouble.

"We'll work something out. Maybe it'll end up being a good time for us both."

# Chapter 11

$\mathcal{I}$ really tried not to think about Joe's comment on making a deposit in my good-time fund. I was supposed to be at a party enjoying myself, practicing my flirtation skills, getting Brad to notice me. But it seemed like I was spending most of my time trying not to think about Joe or something he'd said or done.

If I wasn't thinking about his hazel eyes, or his smile, or the rich timbre of his voice, I was thinking about the way he moved around the hot chocolate counter helping customers with that confident swagger, or the way he'd landed on top of me, or . . .

The way he was totally ignoring me now that we were at the lodge.

He'd slipped away almost as soon as we'd

arrived, getting lost in the crowd. Probably off to make moves on the girl he'd mentioned earlier. Of course, sooner or later, Joe would have to return to my side. After all, I'd promised to dance with him.

"Hey! You made it!" Paige gave me a hug. Her blonde hair was clipped on top of her head, tufts of it sticking out here and there. "Isn't this the best party?"

"Absolutely!"

The lodge was shadowy, with a fire in the massive fireplace providing most of the light. A few candles burned, a few lamps in corners were turned on, but mostly it was shadows.

"The bar's over there, so help yourself."

"Thanks," I said.

"We've got music playing."

"Yeah, I can hear it."

"And dancing over there."

"You don't have to sell me on the party, Paige," I said.

She laughed. "Once a sales clerk, always a sales clerk." Her eyes brightened. "There's the hottie. I'll catch you later."

I watched her head toward Joe, the welcoming smile he gave her, then the way they sauntered over to the dance floor. I wasn't sure why I felt this sudden twinge of loss. It wasn't like she was wrapping herself around Brad.

Brad . . . I needed to find Allie and Leah, then put my plan into action to draw Brad away from Cynthia. Tonight *I* would be the magnet to his sliver of metal.

I wandered through the crowd. I knew most of the nontourists because I came here every winter break, so our paths often crossed. I'd served hot chocolate to many of the tourists. So there was a lot of greeting going on—hey, how are you, good to see you, great powder today—that kind of stuff. I tried not to get bogged down in conversation while I searched for my friends.

I spotted Allie first. She was talking with Sam who had one shoulder pressed to the wall in this am-I-hot-or-what-but-I'm-giving-you-some-time stance. I thought about going to her rescue, but then Sam shoved himself away from the wall, took her hand—took her *hand!*—and led her to the dance area. She really needed rescuing now. I'd seen Sam dance.

But like Leah had said, sometimes you needed to play with the frogs to catch a prince. So maybe that's what Allie was doing. Practicing with my brother so she'd be up for the ski instructors when she finally escaped Sam.

Speaking of ski instructors, that guy dancing with Leah had to be hers. Oh, my gosh. He was to die for! Tall and slender, he had blond hair that fell to his shoulders. He reminded me of models on the covers of romance novels. No wonder she'd pretended to be a klutz in order to have to take the class again. Wow! Good going, Leah!

At least one of us was seriously on our way to finding love on this trip.

I wended my way among the people who were laughing and talking, until I reached the table where all sorts of wintry comfort foods had been laid out. I scooped some clam chowder into a bowl.

"That looks good," I heard Aunt Sue say from behind me.

I looked over my shoulder and smiled. "Want some?"

"Sure do."

I handed her my bowl and filled another bowl for myself.

"Join me by the fire," she said.

At that moment there wasn't anyone I'd rather be talking to—except maybe Brad, who had yet to make an appearance. Considering that Cynthia "loved parties," I'd expected them to be there early.

I sat on a sofa beside Aunt Sue. It was toasty warm in front of the fireplace. I lifted a spoonful of chowder, blew on it to cool it down, then slurped. Really good.

"Having fun?" she asked.

"Having a great time," I lied. "Got Sam to make a donation to the Kate-have-a-good-time fund earlier."

"How did you manage that?" she asked.

"Fooled him into thinking I'd tell Dad he was drinking tonight." I peered over at her. "Don't suppose you want to make a contribution?"

"Katie, you know my philosophy on money."

"It can't buy happiness?"

"No. I work too hard for it to simply give it away."

"Yeah, right." Aunt Sue was always donating boxes of books to libraries and schools across the country, around the world. I knew because I'd helped her lug them to the post office too many times to count. She was always giving in other ways, too.

"What do you need to buy to have a good time?" she asked thoughtfully.

I shrugged. "I'm not sure, but I always like to be prepared." I slurped some more soup.

"Well, when you have a definite goal in mind, let me know and I'll see what I can do."

"I do have a goal. Have fun."

"But you haven't figured out how to achieve that yet."

"Sure I have."

"No, you haven't. Or you wouldn't be sitting here with your old aunt."

"You're not old."

"Getting there."

"So tell me about this guy you almost married."

She laughed her boisterous laughter. "Ah, Katie, why don't you tell me about the guy you're trying to hook up with?"

"I don't think he's here." I looked at her, searching her face for the truth. "Have you seen Brad or Cynthia?"

"So you haven't given up on him?"

"Should I?"

"You tell me."

"You know, you make a lousy Dr. Phil."

She laughed again. "Maybe because I believe we should always listen to our own hearts, and not other people's brains."

"He'd be with me right now, if it wasn't for Cyn," I mumbled. "I just know it."

"Kate, you deserve a guy who'll be with you even if sin—and I'm spelling that S-I-N—is around."

I couldn't help but smile. "I was thinking she should spell her name exactly like that."

"Yeah, I heard you at the pizza place."

"I think Joe did, too." Then I remembered. "We're going to a movie tomorrow night. Did you want to go with us?"

"You don't need a third wheel on your date."

"It's not a date. I asked him and he confirmed that it wasn't a date."

Shaking her head, she gave me a look that

said she thought I was really out of it. "Katie, you don't ask a guy if it's a date."

"Then how would I know?"

"You just know."

"Just know? I'm starting to hate those two little words. Joe uses them all the time." And here I was thinking about Joe again.

"I really like Joe. That was nice of him to help out this afternoon," Aunt Sue said. "And speak of the devil."

With a bright smile, Joe sat on the edge of the coffee table in front of us. I was pretty sure that he was here to make me pay the dance I owed him.

"How's the chowder?" he asked.

"Really tasty." I tapped the bottom of the bowl with my spoon. "But it's all gone. I might have to get some more. Want some?"

"No, thanks." He turned his attention to Sue. "How 'bout you, Sue?"

"No more for me." She patted her stomach. "I'm watching my weight."

"Great! Wanna dance?"

Aunt Sue laughed. "Are you sure I'm the one you want to ask?"

"Absolutely."

With another laugh, Aunt Sue handed me her bowl, stood, and held out her hand. "Then let's go, Casanova."

I watched them walk toward the dance area, and it occurred to me that was pretty much what I'd been doing all night: watching people walk to the dance area, watching people laugh, talk, dance.

I shifted around on the couch to get a better look at the dance floor, and there was Brad and Cynthia. I hadn't been aware that they'd arrived, but there was no missing them now. They were dancing so close and so provocatively that I thought they might get arrested for lewd behavior or something.

I turned back around, set the bowls on the table, and crossed my arms over my chest, trying to hold in the hurt. I had to let Brad go. Just had to.

If I wanted any chance at all of finding love while I was on winter break, I had to completely get over the guy.

# Chapter 12

*A* Brad-ectomy.

That's what I needed.

Without anyone noticing, I left the party and trudged home. After changing into some thick fleece warm-ups, I grabbed the quilt off my bed, made myself a mug of hot chocolate, and curled up in a chair on the redwood deck, the quilt wrapped around me, both hands around the mug, with a mist of steaming chocolate tickling my face.

Our condo looked out over nothing and everything. No houses before me, only trees and hills that grew into mountains. I hadn't turned on any lights, and the houses on either side of me didn't have any on—Cynthia, I knew, was still at the party. Maybe the other neighbors were as well. So it was really dark and quiet. The sky was black and vast, filled with a thousand stars. It was so peaceful and calm.

I breathed it all in: the warmth of chocolate, the scent of trees, the cold of snow. You wouldn't think snow would have a smell, but it does. A pristine crispness in the air.

I took deep breath after deep breath, centering my being, occasionally sipping on chocolate. I started mentally listing all the reasons that I wanted Brad to notice me. The reasons I wanted him for a boyfriend.

*He was hot.*

I tapped my fingernail against the porcelain mug. *Tap. Tap. Tap.*

*He had a killer smile.*

*He was nice.*

*Tap.*

*You don't know that for sure, Kate,* a little voice echoed in my head. I mean, really, what had he done that was nice?

He never talked to me, not really, not like Joe did. He didn't hang around Aunt Sue's bookstore or ask me to go with him to a movie or throw snow at me. He didn't dance with my aunt.

Course, he wasn't dancing with Cynthia, either. What they were doing on the dance floor could hardly be classified as dancing. They'd just been holding each other close like they were trying to keep warm.

*Don't think about it, Kate,* I chastised myself.

Continuing with the Brad-ectomy, I focused on what I really and truly liked about him.

He was hot.

I tapped my mug, sipped my chocolate, tapped my mug.

There had to be something else. I couldn't be this bummed out over a guy not noticing me if he was nothing more than good looks. I wasn't that shallow. Or at least I didn't think I was.

I heard a noise on the stairs and nearly dropped my hot chocolate in my lap.

"Hey, it's just me."

Joe. My breathing slowed, but my heart was still thudding.

"I was knocking on the front door—"

"Sorry, I didn't hear you."

"Not a problem. I thought you were probably back here."

He came up onto the deck and sat in the chair beside mine.

"Why'd you think that?" I asked.

"No reason."

"You must have had a reason."

He shrugged. "Just seemed like the type of place I'd go if I was hurting."

"I'm not hurting," I snapped.

"It's okay, Kate."

"I'm not hurting," I repeated, more irritated with him than imaginable. "I just did a Bradectomy, if you must know."

He chuckled. "A what?"

"I exorcised him. I have no further interest in him whatsoever."

"Really?"

"Yes, really." *Let's move on to another subject.* "Aren't you cold just wearing a leather jacket?"

"You asked me that earlier."

"So? I'm asking again. The later it gets, the colder it gets, so I thought maybe you're starting to get cold now."

"Yeah, I'm starting to get there. Don't suppose you'd share the blanket."

"Nope. I've got it all warm and cozy inside.

Besides, there's not room for the two of us in this chair."

"You'd be surprised."

"Joe, look, you're right. I came here because I wanted to be alone, to just think, so I'm not very good company right now. I don't want to share my blanket—"

"How 'bout your hot chocolate?"

The guy sounded pathetic. I thought I could actually hear his teeth starting to clatter, and I could definitely see his breath on the air. I rolled my eyes. "Sure."

He took my mug and took a swallow. "Just what I needed."

"You can go inside," I told him. "Turn on the fire, watch TV. You don't have to keep me company."

"I've got nothing else to do."

We sat there in comfortable silence for several minutes. Then I peered over at him. "You know Aunt Sue is too old for you."

He laughed, a deep rumble that echoed over the deck. "I don't think she'll ever be old. She has so much energy and so many great stories. I could talk to her all night."

"So why didn't you?" I asked. Even though I really wasn't interested in him as boyfriend material, I think I still wanted him to say that he'd left because of me, because he'd noticed I was gone, because he wanted to be with me. Selfish I know, but there you have it.

"She got a little down after we were talking about Michael and left the party."

I sat up straighter. "Michael? Who's Michael?"

"The guy she almost married."

"She told you his name?"

He looked at me like I'd gone crazy. "Yeah. Why wouldn't she?"

"This morning was the first time I ever heard about him, and she wouldn't tell me anything." Aunt Sue and I were going to have to have a serious sit-down. "Why did she tell you?"

He shrugged again. "Maybe she likes me."

"Did she tell you why she didn't marry him?"

"No, but she did say that his picture's hanging somewhere in her store."

I perked up a little more at that. "I'll break her down in the morning."

"Are you going to work in the shop again?"

"No, but I'll go see her before I head to the slopes. Maybe I can convince her to show me then."

"Maybe."

But he said it like he didn't think I would.

"She was just being her old mysterious self today," I told him. "She'll tell me everything tomorrow."

"If you say so." He stretched out his long legs. "The water in that hot tub sure looks inviting. Have you ever sat in it?"

"No, I'm only ever here in winter. It's too cold to use it then. I don't know why it's not drained. Can you imagine trying to get from the tub into the house while you're wet? You'd turn into a popsicle on the way."

"Might be worth giving it a try. Can you imagine what it would feel like if everything was warm except for your head?"

"It would be weird."

"You think?"

I heard a high-pitched laugh, followed by deeper laughter. Suddenly the lights from Cynthia's condo poured onto her back deck, illuminating her and Brad as they stepped outside. She released an irritating squeal.

"Oh, it's cold!" she cried.

"Well, duh!" I muttered.

She was wearing a bathing suit. And Brad was . . . was he in his boxers?

She pranced across the deck, laughing all the way, until she slid into the hot tub. Brad followed her, raised up on his toes.

"Ah, man!" he yelled, just before he got in the tub.

More laughter, giggling, then silence as they started kissing.

"Don't look at them," Joe ordered.

"It's a little hard not to, if I'm talking to you. They're right in my line of sight."

"Then close your eyes."

Instead I rolled them. "They don't bother me."

"Good. Because I've been thinking about something for most of the night."

I focused on his face, trying really hard not to see past him to where Brad and Cynthia were acting like kids. Yeah, that was it. Kids. Totally immature. Laughing, kissing . . .

"What were you thinking?" I asked.

"Thought I'd make a deposit into the Kate-have-a-good-time fund."

I laughed lightly, appreciating that he was trying to make me feel better. "How much? Five? Ten?"

He shook his head. "Ah, Kate. Like I told you earlier, I'm strapped for cash. I'm talking trade."

He put his hand on the back of my neck, and I had this crazy thought that his fingers should have felt like ice, but they didn't. They were warm.

He pulled me toward him as he leaned nearer, then his lips were on mine and I wasn't thinking at all.

# Chapter 13

*T*here are some things in life that you simply expect.

Like when it snows, you'll get cold, and when you're at the beach, you'll get wet, hot, and sandy. You expect to get gifts at Christmas and presents for your birthday. You expect the sun to come up in the morning and the moon to come out at night. You expect your brother to get on your nerves and your best friends to stick up for you.

You expect life to throw some disappointments at you. You hope it'll throw a few surprises your way.

Joe's kiss was a surprise. Totally, absolutely.

Not so much that he was kissing me. I think in the furthest, farthest corner of my mind, I suspected that he might really like me. That I was the girl he was interested in, the one he'd asked to the movies, even though he'd said it wasn't a date.

So the fact that he was kissing me wasn't that much of a surprise.

What was a surprise was how very good he was at it. At moving his mouth over mine until I wasn't thinking about anything or anyone. I'd been kissed before. I wasn't a complete novice at dating, but Joe took kissing to a whole new level. It was hot and intense, and I imagined the snow around us was probably melting.

And that was fine with me, because I was melting, too, melting right into his arms.

Through the passionate haze, I heard distant voices—not Brad and Cynthia—and a door slam shut.

Joe must have heard it, too, because he pulled back. All I could do was stare at his shadowy face and wonder what he was thinking. If the kiss had been as overwhelming for him as it was for me.

Light suddenly surrounded us as someone inside hit a switch in the living room, and I was vaguely aware of the back door being slid open.

"Hey, what are you guys doing out here?" Leah asked.

"Counting stars," Joe said.

I was certainly seeing stars. I was downright dizzy. And breathless. My lips were tingling.

"Is the party over?" I asked, stupidly.

"Yeah." Leah stepped out onto the deck and gazed off in the direction of Cynthia's condo. "Are they in the hot tub?"

"Yeah."

"That's insane. It's freezing out here."

No, it wasn't. I was quite warm, as a matter of fact.

"Joe was thinking about getting in ours," I said, inanely, anything to deflect attention away from the fact that I might be swaying.

Leah stared at Joe. "Are you nuts?"

"Thought it might be interesting."

How could he sound so normal? Like the kiss hadn't affected him at all? Maybe it hadn't. Maybe, like my crush on Brad, it was all one-sided.

"What might be interesting?" Sam said, as

he and Allie stepped outside.

"Joe was thinking about getting in the hot tub," Leah said.

"Hey, I'm game if everyone else is," Sam said.

"I didn't bring a bathing suit," I said.

"So? Underwear works just as well."

Like I wanted my brother to see me in my undies. Or that I wanted to see him for that matter.

"It's too cold," I said.

"Ah, Kate, you're no fun."

We heard laughter coming from Cynthia's back deck.

Sam looked across the way. "Now, Cyn, she's fun. I bet she never sits on the deck bundled up in a quilt."

Disgusted with my brother, I got up, the quilt still draped around me, my legs shaky. How could they be shaky when I'd been sitting?

"I'm going to bed," I announced.

"You know, Sam, you can be a real jerk sometimes," I heard Joe say once I was inside.

I was halfway across the living room before

Allie caught up with me. "Why didn't you tell us you were leaving the party? We spent half an hour looking for you."

"I didn't get a chance to introduce you to Ian. I really wanted you to meet him," Leah said, coming up to stand beside Allie.

I shrugged. "I just needed to get away for a while."

"You must have seen Brad and Cynthia dancing," Leah said.

"Yeah."

The guys were coming in, too, and I so didn't want my brother to hear any of this.

"I'm going to bed," I repeated. I leaned closer to my best friends. "And Operation Hook-Brad-Up-With-Kate?" Holding the quilt close with one hand, I sliced the other through the air. "It officially ended tonight."

"Are you sure?" Leah asked. "Because I think—"

"I'm sure."

"We'll find you a ski instructor tomorrow," she promised.

Out of the corner of my eye, I saw Joe standing there, watching me, listening.

"Definitely," I said. "Tomorrow Operation Ski Instructor for Kate begins. 'Night."

I walked to my bedroom and closed the door. Getting ready for bed, I could hear the TV on in the living room, and whispered goodnights.

When I finally crawled into bed, I lay there staring at the ceiling, thinking about Joe's kiss. Something for the Kate-have-a-good-time fund.

Kate had definitely had a good time. So good, in fact, that I was slightly terrified. After my experience with Brad, I wasn't sure I could trust my judgment when it came to guys. But I did know one thing.

Joe was just as I'd surmised earlier: dangerous.


"So why would you tell Joe your boyfriend's name and not me?"

Aunt Sue was standing behind her counter at the shop, her morning mug of hot chocolate in one hand, *The Daily Tribune* spread before her. Over her reading glasses, she peered at me like I should have known the answer to the question.

"Gave you something to talk about, didn't it?"

"You told Joe and not me so we'd have something to talk about?"

"That wasn't the original plan, but it just came to me last night at the party."

"So you're playing matchmaker now?"

She smiled mischievously. "No, Kate. I simply gave you something to talk about."

"You know, we do okay on our own."

Boy was that ever an understatement.

"That's good." She went back to reading about the specials at the U-Sack-'Em.

"Did Joe happen to mention me last night while you were dancing?"

"Nope."

I tried not to acknowledge the disappointment by sipping on my own hot chocolate. I guess she took pity on me, because she said, "He talked about you after we danced."

"What did he say?"

"That's between me and him."

"When did you get to be so contrary? You used to tell me everything. And now I find out that you were in love with some guy and you're playing matchmaker and you're keeping conversations secret. You're no fun anymore."

"Because I'm getting old."

The thing I'd learned about older people was that they really no longer cared about impressing others. It made it difficult to bait them or to get your way with them.

"You're not getting old. Joe says you'll never get old."

"Yeah, well, that's because he's young." She looked back at the ad. "There's a special on steaks. Maybe I'll pick some up and cook a meal for all of you."

"We're going to a movie tonight. Remember? Everyone's going. Like I told you last night, it's not a date, so you can come, too."

"I've seen it. I'll have you over for steaks tomorrow."

"Okay. But no matchmaking."

"Wouldn't dream of it."

But the look in her eyes said she was planning to do exactly that.

By the time I got back to the condo, Sam had his car warming up and everyone was clambering inside. Fortunately, I was already dressed for the slopes, so I slid onto the backseat beside Leah, trying really hard not to look at Joe, who was sitting behind her.

We hadn't actually talked since he'd made his deposit in the Kate-have-a-good-time fund, and so I wasn't feeling exactly comfortable around him. I mean, what do you say to a guy who's delivered a kiss as smoothly as he had, a kiss you knew you'd never forget?

Especially if you were wondering if it meant anything.

Allie was in the front passenger seat beside Sam. Sam put the car into gear.

"Aren't we waiting for Brad?" I asked.

"Cynthia, bless her heart, has the sniffles," Leah said.

"And Brad is staying with her today," Allie said.

I supposed I should have admired him for that, but for some reason, he didn't strike me as a heating-up-chicken-soup kinda guy.

Not that it mattered. I was *so* over him.

"Oh," was all I said, like his spending the day with Cynthia absolutely didn't faze me at all. Then I magnanimously added, "Sorry to hear she's not feeling well."

"I guess Operation—"

"Let's not discuss it right now," I said, cutting off Leah and giving her a hard glare.

"Oh, right. Sorry."

"Who's having an operation?" Sam asked, looking at me in the rearview mirror as he drove up the road.

"Sam, she wasn't talking to you," I said.

"Someone's snappish this morning," he said.

"I'm not snappish."

"PMS?"

I ground my teeth together. Where was a snowball when I needed one? I settled back against my seat, folded my arms across my chest, and glared out the window, refusing to address his asinine comment.

"That's so chauvinistic," Leah said.

"Hey, I've lived with her for seventeen years. I know the signs."

"Apparently you don't," I ground out.

"Whatever," Sam said.

"How was your visit with Sue this morning?" Joe asked, leaning forward, his breath skimming the back of my neck.

With my cap pulled down over my head and my jacket zipped up tightly, I was surprised I had any exposed neck at all. But whatever I had, his warm breath found, sending shivers along my spine.

I glanced back at him. He was wearing a deep-blue ski jacket, so his eyes were almost blue. Amazing.

"Obstinate. She wouldn't show me which picture had Michael in it, so maybe we can stop by the shop before we hit the movie and take a look around."

"Who's Michael?" Leah asked.

"The guy I told you about yesterday. The one she almost married. She told Joe his name."

"So we're one step closer to solving the mystery."

"What mystery?" Sam asked.

"When did you get so nosy?"

"Hey, you're talking about my favorite aunt here."

"She's your only aunt."

He chuckled. "Come on, Kate. What's up?"

Before I could say anything else, Allie told him the entire story.

"Huh, I wonder why she didn't marry him," Sam said when Allie was finished.

"She won't say," I said.

"Well, Kate, I'm sure you'll get to the bottom of it," Sam said. "You're her favorite niece, after all."

"At least I'm someone's favorite," I grumbled.

"You're my favorite sister."

I snorted. "Gosh, I'd hate to be your unfavorite. I might not survive."

"Hey, Kate, you know I'm just teasing when I give you a hard time."

"Yeah, right, and the teasing just keeps me laughing."

# Chapter 14

"*I* have to head to class," Leah said brightly. She wiggled her gloved fingers at us. "I'll catch you guys later."

"What's his name again?" I asked.

"Ian. I'll try to introduce you later."

She walked away from us, a definite bounce in her step.

"I'll catch up with you later, too," Allie said. "Sam is going to take me on another ski lift practice run, only this time I'm going to try skiing down one of the easier slopes."

"I can take you on the ski lift," I said, sounding almost desperate in my eagerness not to be left behind.

"That's okay. Sam's going that way anyway, and you should probably do a few runs on the bunny slope, just to warm up since you missed yesterday."

Before I could announce that I didn't need to warm up, she and Sam were trudging through the snow, heads bent toward each other, talking. Talking. Geez, it seemed like every time I looked at them, they were talking. I'd never known my brother to work his jaw so much. He was more of a cut-a-wisecrack-and-run-for-cover kind of guy.

I was sorta feeling like running myself, since I was now alone standing beside Joe.

"Well," I said, clapping my gloved hands together, wondering where we went from here.

"Look, Kate, about that kiss last night . . . it was just a kiss. Nothing to get bent out of shape about."

He and I definitely had a different definition of the word *just*.

Just a kiss was your grandmother pecking your cheek or your nervous prom date pressing his lips to yours so quickly that you weren't even sure they'd actually touched. Joe's kiss had been anything except *just*. It had left absolutely no doubt in my mind that our lips were touching and he wasn't nervous. Nope, he'd been totally in control.

"I'm not bent." Okay I was a little, not so much because he kissed me, but because he didn't seem to be of a mind to kiss me again. "Consider it forgotten," I added, although I knew I wouldn't ever forget it.

"So we're back to being friends?"

How was I supposed to answer that? I'd just met the guy. He was Sam's friend . . . and well, I guess he was becoming mine. "Sure."

"Then you want to buddy-up for the slopes?"

It would have been rude to say no when we were the only two remaining who hadn't buddied up with someone. Besides, it wasn't like he was an irritant like Sam.

I actually enjoyed talking with him. And we won't even go into how I felt about kissing him.

So I smiled at him and said, "Let's go!"

In order to provide support for the ankles, ski boots are pretty sturdy, with very little give, which makes walking in them difficult. So as soon as we got away from the arrival area, we snapped on our skis and headed for the bunny slope.

"I really don't need this practice session," I said. "Skiing is like riding a bicycle. Once you've mastered it, you never forget it."

"Yeah, but it's a good idea to warm up a little before you head for the more advanced slopes. Start the adrenaline rushing, the muscles primed and loosened up."

I was peering at him through my tinted snow goggles. When the snow is pristine white and the sun hits it just right, it can be almost blinding. I'd had more than my share of headaches from not protecting my eyes from that light.

We trudged up to the top of one of the bunny slopes. There was a short line of people waiting their turn to go down it. On another slope, I could see Leah with Ian. Alone.

"Wonder where the rest of the class is?" I mused.

"Actually, he mentioned at the party last night that today was his day off," Joe said.

Which I might have known if I'd hung around the lodge and been a little friendlier with everyone.

I looked over at Joe. "Oh? Is he giving her private lessons?"

He grinned. "I think so. But the lessons may have started last night. They were pretty together at the party."

"Yeah, I saw them. I just didn't realize that . . ." I shook my head. "Doesn't matter. I'm happy for her."

And I was. I really was. I wanted my friends to find love. I wanted them to have an unforgettable time on the slopes.

I was actually beginning to wish that I hadn't spent my first couple of days mooning over Brad. If I'd been here yesterday, I might have found myself with a guy today.

Even as I thought it, I realized that I was with a guy. A fun guy. A nice guy. A hot guy.

While I'd been busy watching Leah, the girl in line behind us had started talking with Joe. I couldn't hear what they were saying, but they were both smiling. I felt my stomach lurch with the realization that I might lose him, too.

Joe turned back to me, his smile still in place.

"Someone you know?" I asked, pleased that my voice sounded pleasantly interested.

"Not before five minutes ago."

I decided to be magnanimous. "If you want to hang out with her—"

"I don't." He nodded. "You're up."

"Up what?"

His grin grew. "Your turn on the slope."

I laughed. "Oh, right. Did you want to go first?"

"Sure."

He got into position, adjusted his goggles, put the tips of his poles into the snow, and shoved off.

He arrived at the bottom of the bunny slope before I even took a breath. Okay. He really did know how to ski. He was standing down there looking up at me. And my nerves were rattled. It had been a year since I'd done this.

The bunny slope was nothing more than a small mound of snow, a starting point for learning the basics. No big deal. I could do this.

I took a deep breath, put my poles into position on the snow, bent my knees, shoved off—

Moving fast with nothing around you is an awesome experience. Even on the bunny slope. The air was cold and whistled by my ears, rushed over my face. There is always a thrill, no matter how many times I ski down a slope. A pitting of my balance and my skills against nature.

Heavy thoughts. But I loved the sensations. The sense of accomplishment.

At the bottom of the slope, I turned my feet so my skis angled slightly, slowing me to a stop in front of Joe. He was grinning.

"You're good."

His praise pleased me more than I thought possible, and I tried not to let it go to my head. It probably had something to do with the battering I'd taken from Brad, even though he hadn't meant to batter me. I was just so not on Brad's radar that he hurt me without meaning to.

"Not as good as you," I said, wanting to return the compliment.

"Don't kid yourself. I had yesterday to practice. Now, let's go have some fun."

And we did have fun. We started on the easier slopes, which like the bunny slope meant we trudged up to the summit, then skied down. Unlike the bunny slope, I didn't have to wait for the person in front of me to reach the bottom. I just let them get started . . . or not. It depended on the width of the trail that I was skiing down. It was always the responsibility of the person behind not to hit the person in front. Just like driving a car.

Only it wasn't always quite as easy to guide your speed. And you had to call out if you were rapidly approaching someone, so they'd know not to swerve over in front of you.

And *swoosh!*

Past them you'd go.

Sometimes you can even race.

Which is what Joe and I started doing after a while. It was amazingly frustrating, because he was really good and he took the competition really seriously. Weaving in and out among a random tree or over a lump of snow that he didn't like the looks of.

I wasn't bad, myself, but I certainly wasn't as good as he was. No matter what he said or how often he complimented my skills.

"Ready to try something a bit more challenging?" he asked, after we'd been at it a couple of hours.

I grinned broadly. "Like Devil's Peak?"

It was the tallest slope that you could reach

using the ski lifts. There was actually a cable car that went up the deepest slope, to the highest peak. But the skiing up there was for the really experienced skiers.

"I'm game if you are," I said.

We headed for the lifts that would take us to the top of Devil's Peak. The chairs on the ski lifts move constantly. We stepped onto the loading platform, just the two of us. A chair swung around and we sat on it while it kept moving forward. There's always this little jerky motion that makes me feel like I might topple out of it.

But somehow I always manage to stay on.

Our skis were on, our feet dangling. I held onto my poles with one hand, onto the ski lift chair with the other.

"I love riding the ski lift," I said.

"Yeah, me, too."

"You can see so much." The ground moving farther and farther away as you went higher and higher toward the summit.

I glanced around at everything surrounding us, the snow-packed trail, the line of trees that ran up either side of the slope, the skiers skiing down, people walking at the edge of the trees, people standing . . .

I leaned forward slightly. I'd recognize the pink coat with the furry collar and cuffs anywhere. "That's Allie," I said, stunned.

"Looks like," Joe said, his voice contained no real surprise, and I wondered exactly what I'd missed out on yesterday. Because she was standing at the edge of the trees, and she wasn't alone. She was with Sam.

Caught in a lip-lock that I thought might require the expertise of the mountain rescue team to break apart.

"I can't believe you were kissing my brother."

Leah, Allie, and I were in my bedroom. It had been difficult, but I'd held my silence on the drive back to the condo. As soon as we got inside, I'd told them that we needed to have a serious talk. So we were all still bundled up and pretty cold. But this conversation couldn't wait.

Allie's cheeks had turned as pink as her jacket. "I can't believe you can't believe it."

"My *brother*," I said with emphasis, in case the snow had blinded her and she hadn't realized exactly who she'd been standing there with. "I don't understand how you could kiss him! I mean, he's . . . he's—"

"Totally hot," Leah interjected.

"*Please!* He is so not hot."

"Oh, he's hot," Leah insisted. "You just don't see it because he's your brother. But he is definitely a hottie."

Dropping down on the edge of my bed, I stared at her, then stared at Allie. "You think he's hot?"

She nodded enthusiastically. "I can't believe you're this surprised. I've had a crush on him forever."

Surprised? I was stunned. "Define *forever*."

"Since I was a junior."

I remembered how she'd offered to share her bedroom with him that first night . . . how breathless she'd sounded, and I'd stupidly thought it was because she was cold. I wanted to bang my head against the wall to knock some sense into myself.

"Oh my gosh. You really *like* him?"

She bobbed her head. "A lot."

"Why didn't you tell me?"

"Because you think he's a jerk. But he's not. I know he gives you a hard time, but that's what brothers are supposed to do."

"How would you know? You don't have any."

She sat on the bed beside me. "He's funny, Kate. He makes me smile, and he has so much patience teaching me how to ski. And his kisses—"

I threw up a hand. "I don't want to hear any details about the game of tonsil hockey you were playing with him."

I looked at Leah. "Did you know they liked each other?"

She smiled. "I suspected she liked him, but I knew Sam liked her. He almost knocked me down to get to the chair across from her at Pile It On Pizza."

"You're kidding? I thought you manipulated the seating arrangement."

"Nope. And he wouldn't let anyone else ride shotgun going or coming from the slopes yesterday or today. Front passenger seat might as well have Allie's name carved on it in gold. And they sat out in the hallway downstairs talking for most of the night."

"About what?"

Allie shrugged. "Anything and everything. We have a lot in common and he's so interesting."

Interesting? Sam?

I tore off my knitted cap and my hair tumbled around my shoulders, flying around in static-electrical wisps. "Brad said that Sam talked about me and Allie on the drive up here. I couldn't figure out why."

"He's liked me for a while, too," Allie said, wearing this dreamy smile.

This was too incredible to believe. How anyone, especially my best friend, could think my brother was boyfriend material was beyond comprehension. My brother! Clueless Sam!

"Kate seems to be speechless," Leah said.

"That's an understatement," I murmured.

"Try to see him from my perspective. He's totally—"

I held up my hand again. "Spare me, please. I will only ever look at Sam like he's my irritating brother." Because that was exactly what he'd always be to me. I would certainly never contemplate him as hot. That was too gross.

I glanced over at Allie. "You'll always be my best friend, though. Even if I question your sanity."

She grinned. "So we're all going to the movie together tonight, right?"

"Not me," Leah said. "I'm meeting Ian at the Avalanche."

The Avalanche was a little of everything: a sports bar with live entertainment.

"Sounds like you're serious about this guy," I said.

"I'm getting there."

"Which leaves me with no one," I said. A total downer.

"Looked like you had someone last night . . . on the deck," Leah said. "Or was it just an optical illusion that made it look like you were kissing Joe?"

I felt the heat rush to my face. I wasn't cold anymore.

"I wasn't kissing him. He was kissing me, but he said it's no big deal."

"Yeah, sure. It certainly looked like a big deal."

"I don't even know how you could see us.

We were in the dark."

"You were a shadowy silhouette. Trust me, we saw."

Which meant Sam saw, too. I couldn't believe he hadn't said anything. Probably because it would have embarrassed his friend. Not because he wanted to spare me any mortification. Sam didn't work that way. At least not where I was concerned.

Not wanting to follow this trail of conversation any further, I stood up and unzipped my jacket. "I need to get ready for the movie."

"Your big date?" Leah said, wiggling her eyebrows.

"No, we're just friends."

"I don't kiss my friends."

"Will you let it go?" I asked. "He knows how I feel about Brad. He's not making any moves on me."

"If you say so."

Honestly, my friends were becoming as irritating as my brother.

"I like him better than I like Brad," Allie said.

"It doesn't matter," I said. I made a little

waving motion with my hands. "Now, go, so we can all get ready."

Once they left, I dropped back down onto the edge of my bed, stared at the floor between my snow boots.

Having everyone witness my failure with Brad hadn't been fun. Even though I trusted Allie and Leah with everything . . . I wasn't quite ready to admit that maybe I was falling for Joe . . . just a little.

Brad was a player. For all I knew, Joe was, too.

I mean, really, why had he kissed me?

How did a girl know when she could trust a guy not to break her heart?

# *Chapter 15*

"*W*hat about this one?" I asked, pointing to a picture of Aunt Sue standing beside a man with a camera slung around his neck. They both wore safari hats and brown clothing. The foliage was thick behind them. I thought it was taken during one of her trips to Africa, because a guy who was about eight feet tall was also standing beside her. A tribal chief, I thought.

"Nah, he doesn't look like a Michael," Joe said.

We'd decided to stop by A Novel Place on our way to the movie to see if we could locate the mysterious love of Aunt Sue's life. Sam and Allie were going to meet us at the Last Buck. Leah was meeting Ian at the Avalanche. Brad had been AWOL at supper, which was a shame because the stew had been really delicious—a little short on vegetables, though. Now I knew why Allie was so keen on fixing it the way that Sam wanted it.

"What does a Michael look like?" I asked.

Joe shrugged. He was wearing a bulky green sweater that made his eyes turn green. I was wearing a green sweater as well, but my eyes would have looked green regardless.

"We'll know him when we see him," he assured me.

So far, we'd looked at about two dozen pictures. The most difficult part was that they were spread throughout the store with no rhyme or reason. Some hanging on the walls, some displayed on bookshelves. Some were just of Aunt Sue. Most had someone else in them, but seldom the same person. There was no pattern, no one who always showed up.

"Maybe he was the one always taking the pictures," I muttered.

"She said there was a picture of him here."

I looked around. There were so many nooks and crannies. A Novel Place had a lot of novel places that displayed various items.

It was almost like being in a room of mirrors where all the mirrors reflected all the other mirrors into infinity. I got dizzy just thinking about it.

Joe glanced at his watch. "If we want to make the beginning of the movie, we're going to have to go."

I took a last look around the bookstore. Paige was behind the register counter, but Aunt Sue was nowhere to be found. Probably off at the U-Sack-'Em buying steaks for tomorrow. I needed to tell everyone we were doing that tomorrow night. I'd see Aunt Sue in the morning and tell her about Ian, because he'd probably join us. And I'd *make* her show me the picture of Michael.

"Okay," I said. "Let's go."

It wasn't a far walk to the Last Buck. Sam and Allie were standing out there waiting for us.

"They changed movies," Allie said.

Joe looked at the marquee and groaned. They were now showing a chick flick.

"I say we blow off the movie and head to the Avalanche," Sam said.

"Sounds good to me," Joe said.

I considered the options. Sitting in the dark with Joe, while Sam and Allie got it on beside us — I wasn't naive enough to think my brother wouldn't take advantage of the dark — or head to a place with pretty much the same offerings that we had last night. The Avalanche would at least provide an opportunity to mingle with people.

I glanced at Allie and could see that her mind was made up. Whatever Sam wanted, she wanted. And I hadn't really wanted to go to a movie, anyway.

"I'm okay with the Avalanche," I said.

So off we went, with all our gloved hands stuffed into our jacket pockets. To see us, no one would guess that at least two of us were a couple.

What was up with that, anyway?

In the main area, the Avalanche had a live band playing. The Ski Lifts.

I don't know if that was the band's real name or if that was just the name they used when they played at ski resorts. I mean, I couldn't exactly see them ever making an appearance on David Letterman with a name like that.

Like Paige and her bookstore name.

"That isn't her real name, by the way," Joe said.

We'd joined Leah and Ian at their table. Ian did have a delicious accent.

"It's good to meet you, mates," he'd said, his Australian accent thick. "My sheila talks about you all the time."

I'd shaken my head. Couldn't any of these guys get the names right?

"Her name is Leah," I'd said, knowing how it hurt to have a guy call you the wrong name.

"*Sheila* is what they call girls in Australia," Leah said, a look of adoration on her face. "He's saying that I'm his girl."

"Come on, Leah love," he'd said then. "Let's dance."

*Leah love?* How adorable. I could see why she was falling for this guy. They moved to the dance floor. Allie and Sam went to the back room where there were Foosball tables and a TV showing a football game. Leaving me and Joe to guard the table from the tourists who were searching for a place to sit. The place was crowded tonight.

I stared at Joe, trying to figure out what he'd been trying to say. "What?"

"Paige Turner. That's not her real name."

"How did you know I was thinking about Paige?"

Shaking his head, he grinned. "I didn't. I was just watching the Ski Lifts, thinking that a band with such a bland name would never show up on Letterman—"

"Oh, my gosh, that's *exactly* what I was thinking."

His grin grew. "Really?"

Too bizarre. I nodded.

"Great minds, huh?"

I returned his smile. "I guess so."

"Well, anyway, thinking of the band's name reminded me about Paige, and since we'd talked about her being in the witness protection program," he shrugged, "I forgot to tell you that I asked her last night about her name."

"She's not in the witness protection program, is she?" I asked, somewhat disappointed that I was going to have to give up on my theory.

"Nope. She's an official member of the what-were-my-parents-thinking-when-they-named-me club."

I couldn't help but chuckle at that. "So what did they name her?"

"She wouldn't say."

"Bummer! Why is everyone being so secretive this year? Aunt Sue and now Paige."

"She said she'll only tell her husband and only after they've been married for a while."

I laughed. "Well, I guess you could offer to marry her in order to learn her deep, dark secret."

"Even talking marriage makes me break out in hives. That is so far down on my to-do list that I might never get to it."

"Mine, too." I shook my head. "Poor Paige. So she went to work in a bookstore and decided to change her name to Paige Turner. What a hoot."

"Yeah, I thought so."

I sipped on my warm apple cider. Even though I'd already told him that Paige thought he was hot, considering the "just a kiss" he'd given me last night, I thought I should remind him that he had options. "She really likes you, you know."

He looked down at the table. "Yeah, I know. She wasn't too shy about making that clear last night when we were dancing."

Then he peered over at me, like what he wasn't saying was more important than what he had said. And maybe it was. Because he knew Paige liked him, and there was the girl at the ski lift that he could have hooked up with, and yet here he was with me.

So now I had to ask myself: What are you going to do about it, Kate?

"How important do you think guarding this table is?" Joe asked.

I leaned closer to him. My thoughts had drifted off and I wasn't exactly sure where he was going with this. "What?"

"I'm starting to feel like the dullest guy at the resort. I mean, we've got dancing over there, Foosball in the back room, and I'm sitting here guarding a table."

"If we leave it unguarded, it'll probably get taken hostage by one of these unsavory-looking tourists," I said.

"Probably."

"On the other hand, what are we saving it for?"

"Exactly. I've got a hankering for a little Foosball action."

Okay, I have to admit that I was a little disappointed. I was hoping for a dance, close up and personal. But I may have blown my opportunity for that because I hadn't hung around the lodge last night.

Or maybe Foosball would be the warm-up.

"I'm wicked awesome at Foosball," I said. Sam had gotten a Foosball table one year for Christmas. He'd set it up in our game room back home.

"Great! Then let's get wild."

We'd barely moved away from our chairs before someone was knocking up against the table and asking, "You guys leaving?"

I looked at Joe, who just shrugged.

"Yeah," I told the guy. He started waving frantically for his friends.

Joe and I wended our way through the mass of bodies and finally arrived at the gaming room. A TV was set near the ceiling in each of the four corners. The volume was turned down to a tolerable level so multitasking could take place. Games played, conversations going on.

Unfortunately, this room was as crowded as the other room. Not an empty Foosball table to be found. So maybe I was going to get that dance after all.

"What now?" I asked.

"Let's watch Sam and Allie," he suggested.

Oh, yeah, good idea. That's really how I wanted to spend my evening.

Joe led the way and I followed. When we got to the table, Sam called a time out.

"Hey, what're you guys doing?" he asked.

"Not much," I said.

"Want to play teams?" he asked. "Guys against girls?"

"Sure, why not?" I said.

I took my place beside Allie, near the goal. Joe stood across from me and beside Sam.

"Okay, rules," Sam announced. "No spinning the rods. Best of nine."

He picked up the small ball. "Everybody ready?"

I took hold of two of the rods, spun them,

bent my knees, rolled my shoulders, got into position. Tapped my elbow against Allie's. She grinned at me. I had a feeling she might have been holding back while she played with Sam. Either that or he had vastly misjudged my skill at this game.

Sam gave his eyes an exaggerated roll and released a deep breath.

Vastly misjudged it was!

"Ready!" I announced.

Sam dropped the ball down the chute and it rolled onto the center of the table. Allie tapped it toward my end of the table. And as soon as it was in position, I fired it into the hole.

"Score!" I yelled, giving Allie a high five.

Sam looked dumbfounded. He shook his head. "Beginner's luck."

He took the ball, dropped it down the chute—

Allie hit it, Joe hit it, Allie stopped it, hit it my way, I smacked it—

"Score!" I shouted, and Allie and I exchanged another high five.

Sam shoved Joe's shoulder. "You're letting her score!"

"I'm not *letting* her do anything."

"Trade places."

Sam got into position and glared at me. "Let's see how good you are with a pro across from you."

Joe dropped the ball down the chute, Sam made first contact, I made second, third—

"Score!"

"Have you been practicing with my Foosball table at home?" Sam asked.

Grinning broadly, I said, "You bet!"

"I didn't give you permission—"

"Like I need it. You should see the things I do in your room."

"You mess in my room?"

I reached across the table and patted his shoulder. "I'm teasing, Sam. The only thing Allie and I touch is the Foosball table. And a few of your CDs."

He looked at Allie. "Were you letting me win earlier?" he asked suspiciously.

"No, I'm just better when I'm with Kate."

"Switch places," Sam ordered me.

"What are we doing, playing musical partners here?"

He took my arm and pulled me around the table until I was beside Joe and he was beside Allie. "I didn't know we were playing with Foosball sharks here. We're starting over."

"You're a sore loser, Sam," I said.

Joe leaned toward me. "You want to be at the goal end?"

"I'd love to be at the goal end, but I'd rather face Sam. I'll warn you, though, Allie's sneaky. Don't let her fool you."

"No giving away secrets," Allie said, smiling.

"Let's play!" I said, feeling invigorated and ready to kick some butt.

The teams were much better matched with the new arrangement. Of course, I had a secret weapon. I kept pretending the little ball was Brad and I was actually kicking his butt for being such a jerk. It felt good to unleash my anger and disappointments completely, much better than meditating him out of my system.

And even though I'd done the Brad-ectomy the night before, this final exercise was refreshing. I wasn't moping about him. I was actually enjoying myself.

By the time Joe and I won two out of three games, Sam decided he'd had enough and was making rumblings about hauling his Foosball machine to college. I'd seen his dorm room. Finding a place for the table wasn't going to happen.

"How 'bout some air hockey?" Joe asked.

"Sure."

A table had opened up and we grabbed it. Joe put the coins in to release the puck and start the air blowing. I closed my hand around the paddle and swept it over the table a couple of times.

Joe slid the puck toward me. "You start."

I smacked it, he smacked it back. I love air hockey more than Foosball. The puck can go so fast and it makes this terrific smacking sound. It's great for relieving stress or tension. I was feeling pretty relaxed—

"Score!" I shouted as the puck slipped through the slot at Joe's end of the table.

Joe grabbed the puck, set it on the table, and . . . smack!

Right into the slot at my end of the table. He wiggled his brows and gave me a cocky grin.

*All right,* I thought to myself. *A little competition.*

I put the puck into play and we were going back and forth, hitting it hard . . .

"You're really competitive, aren't you?" Joe asked.

"You bet!"

*Smash, score!*

I smiled saucily. "I like to win."

"I figured that out this afternoon on the slopes whenever we'd race."

"Yeah, but you always won there."

"I like the fact that you didn't pout about it."

He hit the puck hard and I couldn't stop it from going into the slot. I picked up the puck.

"I recognize skill when I see it."

I slammed the puck hard, but he still stopped it, sent it back my way. I sent it back his. He hit. I hit.

He scored.

I set us up for another volley.

"You know, you still owe me a dance," Joe said. And scored.

Not fair. He'd distracted me.

"Yeah, I guess I do." I scored.

"So how 'bout we dance after I beat you here?"

*Smack! Score!*

"How 'bout we dance after I beat *you*?"

He gave me that warm, cute grin of his. "Works for me."

We went back and forth, the score always close, but he won, by one point. I was exhausted and breathing heavily by the time we were finished. And there was a line of people not so subtly breathing down our necks waiting to have their turn at the table.

Joe sauntered around the table until he reached me. He put his hand on the small of my back, and just like last night when he'd kissed me, I could tell it was warm. The heat seeped through my sweater.

"Let's go," he said.

He escorted me through the crowd until we reached the dance floor. The Ski Lifts were playing a fast-paced song.

Joe and I started dancing. It was strange, because we weren't touching, we were each kinda in our own little space. But the way Joe held my gaze the entire time, it was almost like there was an invisible thread pulling us toward each other.

And I couldn't help but wonder if I wasn't a little like Dorothy from *The Wizard of Oz*, searching far and wide for something that had been in my backyard the entire time.

# Chapter 16

$\mathcal{I}$t was late by the time we all got home—all being Leah, Allie, Sam, Joe, and me. Brad was still missing in action, playing nurse at Cynthia's.

After I got ready for bed, I had way too much on my mind to actually settle into sleep. I was still in semi-shock over Sam and Allie, although it sure hadn't seemed like they were hooked up at the Avalanche. I mean, they danced together, played Foosball together, sat together, and talked together, but they weren't all over each other—not like Cynthia and Brad had been the night before, anyway. And Sam kept looking at me like he was doing something he shouldn't, something that I should tattle on.

And then there was Joe. Good-time Joe who made me laugh and smile. I liked him. A lot.

When things got really quiet in the condo and all I could hear was the moaning of the wood as the house settled in for the night, I put on my robe, grabbed my quilt, and tried to slip out of my room unnoticed.

But Joe was still up, the TV on, the volume turned down way low. I didn't even know how he heard it.

"I'm going out on the deck," I whispered. "To be alone."

Which I knew made no sense because I'd been alone in my room. But I preferred to do my heavy thinking on the deck.

"Not a problem," he said, graciously taking the hint to leave me alone and turning his attention back to the TV.

I almost asked him to join me. I thought if I told him that I didn't really want to be alone, but that I needed to think, that he would sit out there and not say a word. From the moment I'd met him, Joe seemed like he always knew exactly what I needed and how I needed him to give it to me. Whether it was silence or conversation or teasing or a kiss.

And while I didn't *want* to be alone, I thought

I *needed* to be alone. At least for a little while so I could sort out my thoughts.

I crossed the room, unlocked the sliding glass door, and stepped out onto the deck. I wrapped my quilt around myself and curled up in the chair. I dared to glance over at Cynthia's condo. No one frolicking in the hot tub. Thank goodness.

I blinked as a snowflake landed on my eyelash. Then noticed that others were falling. We'd have fresh powder come morning. I snuggled down more deeply in my quilted cocoon.

Then I saw a shadow and Brad was suddenly standing on the back deck, rubbing his arms. He was wearing clothes, but no jacket. Was he crazy? And where had he come from and how long had he been out there?

"Hey, I'm so glad someone is still up. Is it okay if I go in and get my stuff? I'm going to move in with Cyn for the duration."

I thought I should have felt a pang in my heart, but I didn't. I didn't feel anything. Maybe my heart had turned to ice.

"Sure. But I gotta warn you, Sam gets mean when he gets woken up."

"Tell me about it. I know all about his sleeping habits."

He slipped inside and I bundled myself up tighter, studying the night. It was strange, but I thought I really was over him. Maybe it had been a little silly to crush on him as much as I had. I mean really. What did we have in common? Nothing except my brother. Not exactly heavy-duty bonding material.

The door opened again and Brad stepped out, holding his duffle bag. "Thanks a lot, Allie."

I grimaced not for the first time at the realization that he couldn't remember my name, then decided I was definitely over the guy. "You're welcome, Bart."

"Brad."

"Kate."

"Huh?"

I wanted to laugh. "I'm Kate."

"Oh, right. Right. Kate's the sister. Allie's the friend. Man, there are way too many chicks here. Never thought I'd say this, but I'm glad that I'm hot-footing it next door where there's only one. Later."

With that, he turned and hurried down the steps.

Hearing the door behind me slide open again, I shook my head. No doubt Joe coming to make sure I was all right, that I had survived Brad's nighttime visitation with my heart intact. But when I looked over my shoulder, it wasn't Joe. It was Sam.

He sat in the chair beside me. "Geez, it's freezing out here. And it's snowing! Give me a part of that quilt, will ya?"

"Go get your own."

"Come on, Kate. Play nice."

"Why? You never do." Still, I shifted in my chair and freed up one end of the quilt. He moved his chair closer to me. The quilt was a king size so I could share a little of it.

"You okay?" he asked quietly.

"Sure. Why wouldn't I be?"

"Brad. I know you were crushing on him, and now he's packed it up and moved next door. I wanted to make sure you weren't having trouble dealing with it."

"I can't believe Allie told you about my crush."

"Give me a break, Kate. I've known since family weekend. When was the last time you wanted to take a picture of me? Document my freshman year? What? Do I have clueless tattooed across my forehead?"

Narrowing my eyes, I leaned toward him. "Yeah, I think maybe you do."

Even in the shadows, I could see him grin. This was so totally weird. Sitting out here, having an almost normal conversation with my brother.

"He's not your type, Kate."

I scoffed. "How do you know my type? I don't even know my type."

"Trust me, when you do figure your type out, you're gonna realize it's not Brad. I mean, I like him, and he's a great roommate, but what I want in a friend and what you need in a boyfriend aren't the same. He'd just end up hurting you. Then I'd have to beat the crap out of him."

I couldn't stop myself from smiling. "Would you really do that for me, Sam?"

"You know I would." His voice was totally serious.

And I realized that he was so not joking. His revelation stunned me almost as much as Joe's kiss. No, wait, nothing would ever throw me off balance as much as that kiss.

"You do know that, don't you, Kate?" Sam asked. "You're my sister and I . . ." He waved his hand. "That L-word. You know."

"Love?" I asked.

"Don't make me say it, okay? Just know it's true. I know I give you a hard time, but hey, that's what brothers do. It's part of our genetic makeup, a little chip inside our brains that gets activated when our parents shove a screaming baby sister in our face."

"Like you'd have a memory of that moment. You were only fifteen months old."

"Whatever. Look, I'm out here right now because I've been a little worried about you, and I haven't really been able to get you alone to talk."

"You've been able to get Allie alone." And for a lot more than conversation.

He grimaced. "Yeah, she told me you know about us. Are you okay with that?"

"What if I'm not?"

"Then tough. Get over it."

"Some understanding brother you are."

"I've got my limits."

"So you really like her, huh?"

"Yeah. I have for a long time, but geez, she's my sister's best friend. How weird is that?"

"Totally weird. When she described the way you kiss—"

"What?" Horror echoed in his voice. His eyes were wide, his mouth open.

"Payback for the snowball," I said snidely.

"I already paid you back for that."

"So? Maybe there's a little chip inside a girl's brain that gets activated when her brother is a jerk and erases paybacks as soon as they happen so we need a steady stream of them."

"You're definitely not playing nice, Kate." I heard him heave a sigh. "You know, that's part of the reason I've steered clear of Allie. I don't want her discussing my . . . moves with my sister."

"Yeah, like you've got moves."

He gave me a cocky look. "Hey, I've got moves."

I held up my hand. "Definitely don't want to hear about them."

"Definitely don't want you to hear about them." He leaned forward, planted his elbows on his thighs, and peered at me. "Seriously, you're okay with me and Allie?"

"I question her taste in guys, but yeah, I'm okay. Is that the reason you weren't acting like a couple tonight? Because you thought it would freak me out?"

"I was a little uncomfortable. Stupid, I know. But it's a little strange liking someone who stays up all night whispering to my sister about personal things. I mean, admit it. You talk a lot about guys."

"Sure, we do, but not the really personal stuff. She won't reveal your secret handshake."

"It's not my handshake I'm worried about."

"Pretend it is, because as far as I'm concerned, that's all the two of you do. Shake hands. Even if I see you kissing? In my head, I'm going to tell myself that you're shaking hands."

"I guess that'll work. And you sure you're okay that Brad moved next door?"

I shrugged. "I need more than what he was offering."

"You know, Kate, I'm here for you if you ever need me."

The strange thing was, I knew he meant it. Sure, he was usually clueless, but he was my brother, and I knew he loved me—as much as I loved him.

"Thanks, Sam."

He stood up and tucked the part of the quilt he'd borrowed around me.

"Don't stay out here too long. Don't want to find you here in the morning, a frozen statue. Who'd cook me breakfast?"

"I love you, Sam."

"Course you do." He gave me his usual arrogant grin. "What's not to love?"

Before I could start listing all the things, he disappeared into the condo, leaving me alone with my thoughts. I realized there were times when Sam wasn't half bad as a brother.

So maybe I could understand why Allie had hooked up with him. Of course, I'd never tell him that!

# Chapter 17

There are days on the mountain when it's so sunny and so bright, the sky is such a clear blue, that you almost forget it's winter. Your face gets sunburned, sometimes worse than it would at the beach because the sunshine reflects off the snow. It's like being surrounded by a tanning lamp set on high. But the bite in the air and the way your lungs ache if you breathe too deeply always serve to remind you that it's not summer.

Then there are days when the wind howls down through the mountain passes and you understand how myths about Bigfoot first began. People had to feel like they were afraid of more than the wind.

"No hot tub tonight," Joe said, like he thought someone was possibly considering it.

We were all nestled inside the condo: Joe, Allie, Sam, Ian, Leah, Aunt Sue, and me. The first sign of the storm was when the sky had darkened and the wind had picked up enough to close down the ski lifts and gondolas. Trust me, you don't want to be on either one when the winds are strong enough to rock them. Even if the cables hold, your heart might not. It's frightening.

The increasing strength of the winds and the poor visibility had the slopes closing down. So like all the other skiers, we'd headed back at a slow crawl.

Aunt Sue had closed up her shop and had been inside the condo, setting out candles and supplies—just in case—when we arrived. The look of relief on her face had me apologizing for not calling to let her know that we were all fine and on our way back.

"It always seems when they predict bad weather, it doesn't happen," she said. "It's when they don't predict it and it happens that you have to watch out."

"Are you going to stay with us tonight?" I asked.

"We'll see," she said. "At least through supper."

She'd brought over the steaks she'd bought and cooked them in the broiler instead of out on a grill. They really hit the spot.

Supper had been an hour ago, and everyone was still here. Waiting it out. We had the drapes pulled back on the sliding glass doors, and the outside light on. Not that we could see much except swirling snow and accumulation.

"How much snow are we supposed to get?" Sam asked. He and Allie were sitting on the couch, holding hands.

"They're predicting two feet," Aunt Sue said.

"Two feet?" Allie asked. "How will we get out in the morning?"

"Just open the door and start plowing your way through," Ian said.

Leah smiled at him like he was her own personal hero. I guess he was. He'd brought her back from the mountains. They'd been riding on the gondola that went up to the highest peak when I'd called her on my cell. She'd told us to go ahead and not wait on her. So Ian had brought her home and joined us for supper.

"At least there's a football game on tonight," Sam said.

"Yeah, but in about twenty minutes, the girls get the TV," I said.

Sam groaned. "Ah, come on, Kate. We're in the middle of a snowstorm here. I can't go down to the Avalanche and watch their TV."

I lifted my shoulders in a hapless shrug. "Sorry, but rules are rules."

"What are you going to watch?"

"Something you'll hate."

"Great."

Aunt Sue was sitting in a recliner, Joe in the other. Leah, Ian, and I were sitting on these big floor pillows in front of the fire.

Joe got out of his chair. "I'm going to get something to drink. Anyone want anything?"

"Kate, why don't you and Joe make us all some hot apple cider?" Aunt Sue asked.

While I sneaked a glare at Aunt Sue, Joe said, "That sounds good. If you'll just tell me how—"

"It's easier if she shows you," Aunt Sue said.

"She's right," I said, as I shoved myself to

my feet and whispered, "Meddlesome match-maker," in her ear as I walked by.

She just laughed while I followed Joe into the kitchen.

"Did I miss a joke?" Joe asked, when I came into the room.

I was really embarrassed that Aunt Sue was being so obvious about what she was trying to do. If I didn't know better, I'd think she arranged this snowstorm just so we'd all have to stay indoors for a while.

"Not really," I said. "Just Aunt Sue giving me a hard time. Grab the mugs, will you?"

I went to the pantry and pulled out the box of hot apple cider mix. Then I went to a cabinet, took out a pan, poured water into it, and set it on the stove to heat. Joe had placed an assortment of mugs on the counter. I dipped a spoonful of powder into each one.

"Tell me there's more to it than just adding water," he said.

I gave him a pointed look. "Nope. That's all there is to it."

He looked over his shoulder at the door-way that led to the living room, then back at me. "Matchmaking?"

I grimaced and nodded.

"You don't look thrilled."

"It's my love life, and everyone treats it like it's a community project."

"That's because they care about you."

"And I appreciate it. I just . . ." I shook my head. "I just wish everyone didn't know I made a fool of myself with Brad."

"You didn't make a fool of yourself."

"I'd really prefer not to talk about it."

And I wished he wasn't being so nice about it, which was a dumb thing to wish. I took the pot of boiling water off the stove and began pouring the water into the mugs.

"Stir," I ordered.

"Yes, ma'am," he said like a private answering a drill sergeant.

"Sorry, I don't mean to take it out on you."

"Not a problem."

He started stirring. I emptied the pot, rinsed it out, and put it in the sink. I grabbed the box of mix and carried it back to the pantry. Something caught my eye. "Hey!"

"What?"

I hadn't heard him approach, but Joe was right there, in the pantry doorway with me.

"Do you like s'mores?"

"Love s'mores."

I held up a box of graham crackers and a package of chocolate bars. "I was a girl scout."

"And I was a boy scout, but we have no campfire—"

We also suddenly had no lights. I heard a couple of shrieks, some male laughter, a couple of *shhh's*.

And my heart pounding.

"Joe?"

"Yeah?"

I released a nervous chuckle. "It's really dark."

"Yeah."

In the distance I heard, "Where's the flashlights?"

"I thought we had flashlights."

"Someone light a candle."

Joe said quietly, "There's a little light in the other room because of the fireplace."

"We should probably move in there then."

"Probably so."

But we both just continued to stand there. My eyes had adjusted and I could see his outline, just standing there. I'd crushed the box of graham crackers and chocolate against my chest.

"We should find the marshmallows first," I said.

"I think s'mores are out. We have no electricity."

"But we have a fire. We could stick marshmallows on a coat hanger."

"A true girl scout," he said.

I felt his hand wrap around my neck, felt his breath skim along my cheek.

"How did you find me?" I asked.

"Just did."

Probably by the rapid pounding of my heart. I thought I could hear it echoing throughout the pantry.

"Kate?"

"Yeah?"

"Is the Brad-ectomy holding?"

"Totally."

I felt his lips brush mine —

"Everybody okay in here?" It was Sam,

yelling, sweeping the light of the flashlight around the room, startling me.

Joe stepped back quickly. I wanted to toss the cookies at my brother.

"We're fine, Sam," I said. "It's just a loss of power. No reason to overreact."

There was a flickering and the lights came back on.

"What are y'all doing in there?" Sam asked, his gaze narrowed as it went from Joe to me.

Ah, suspicious minds.

I held up the box and bag of goodies. "Searching out s'more makings."

"Cool! I love s'mores."

Everyone loved s'mores. Allie went into my bedroom and found some hangers, which the guys uncoiled. There wasn't enough room in front of the fireplace for everyone so—surprise, surprise!—the girls were the designated cooks.

I skewered a marshmallow and warmed it over the fire. I wanted it to be a perfect golden brown.

I looked over my shoulder. We'd set the graham crackers broken in half on a cookie tray and set the chocolate bars on half of them. Although now little evidence remained that chocolate had ever been there. "Sam! Stop eating the chocolate!"

All three guys were guiltily licking their fingers, but you can't get after guys you barely know, so Sam got the brunt of my yelling.

"It's taking too long to make these things," he said.

I grabbed the bag of chocolate bars and moved it to the other side of me.

"Hey, your marshmallow's on fire," Joe said.

"Dadgum it!" I pulled it close and blew on it. It was charred, and gravity was drawing the melting ooze toward the floor. I dropped it on a graham cracker, snatched a chocolate bar out of the bag, unwrapped it, broke it in half, and placed it on top of the marshmallow, then a cracker on top.

The three guys were waiting to see who I'd favor with the s'mores. And since Sam had Allie and Ian had Leah . . . well, I had no choice. I held it out to Joe.

He grinned, took the offering, and promptly

wolfed it down. "Thanks, but try not to burn the next one."

I scowled at him. He laughed.

"It's gonna be a long night," I said.

It was a long night. The lights went out again, but we were prepared with the candles already lit and flashlights nearby.

We were also all stuffed with s'mores. I thought if I never saw another marshmallow for the rest of my life, it would be too soon.

"Well, this sucks," Sam said, sitting on the floor, his back against the couch. "I wonder how the game ended."

"Someone won, someone lost," I said.

"Very funny, Kate." He glanced over at Aunt Sue who was reading a book in the recliner, using a tiny flashlight. "You're not going to try to walk home tonight, are you?"

Looking up, she peered out the glass doors. "Probably not."

"You can sleep with me," I offered. "I've got the king-size bed."

"Thanks, Katie."

"It'll be like old times," I said. When I was little, I'd always sleep with Aunt Sue when I came to visit her.

Aunt Sue smiled. "Do you remember that time—"

"Aunt Sue, before you say something that will probably embarrass me, can we skip the walk down memory lane?"

"If you insist."

"There will be great skiing tomorrow," Ian said.

"Since Brad moved out and we have the extra bed downstairs, I told Ian he could stay. I hope that's okay," Leah said.

"That's cool," Sam said.

"He can sleep on the couch, Joe, if you want—" Leah began.

"I'm cool on the couch."

Leah smiled like Joe had handed her a ring. I guess she wanted Ian as close as she could have him.

"How long have you lived here, Ian?" Aunt Sue asked.

"Three years."

"Do you miss your family?" Allie asked.

"A little, but I love living here. America has the most beautiful girls." He gave Leah a look that said she was one of them.

"I always thought Australian girls were beautiful," Sam said.

Allie slapped his arm.

"Hey!" He rubbed his arm. "What was that for?"

"You're not supposed to notice beautiful girls."

"I was doing the noticing before you."

I couldn't help but smile. Allie always seemed like the quietest of our group, but I had a feeling that Sam wasn't going to get away with a whole heck of a lot.

I felt Joe's gaze on me and I looked over at him. I think he was thinking the same thing. That Allie was sweet, but she also knew her own mind.

"I think I'm going to turn in," Aunt Sue said. "Good skiing tomorrow means I'll be busy in the morning. Goodnight, everyone."

Her departure practically started a stampede: the downstairs group headed downstairs, leaving me and Joe sitting in front of the fireplace, watching the fire burn. I thought about saying that I should go to bed, too, but I wasn't tired.

The lights came back on and Joe popped up. "I'm going to turn them all off."

We left the candles burning. The scent was familiar. I remembered it from that first morning when I'd done meditation with Aunt Sue. I was pretty sure it was midnight passion.

Figured. She probably hadn't really gone to bed, either. Come to think of it, she took her book with her. Meddlesome matchmaker.

Joe sat back down on the floor. Raised a knee, draped his wrist over it, looked at the fire.

"Well, I guess when the storm is over and Ian goes back to wherever he lives, you'll finally get to sleep in a bed," I said.

"I like the couch."

"How can you like sleeping on the couch?"

He angled his head slightly so he could see me better. "I just do. I can watch TV, raid the kitchen."

"You raid the kitchen?"

"Sometimes."

Of course, he could still watch TV and raid the kitchen if he was sleeping in a bed. It wasn't like where he slept made either off-limits.

I thought about what had almost happened

in the pantry, how he'd almost kissed me. Part of me wanted to say, "Hey, remember what we were doing before Sam spoiled the party? You can finish now."

But part of me thought that maybe I should leave well enough alone. I'd practically thrown myself at Brad. I didn't want to do that with Joe.

I mean, sure, he'd expressed some interest and maybe he had wanted to kiss me earlier, but he didn't seem to want to kiss me now. I drew my legs up, wrapped my arms around them, planted my chin on my knees, and stared at the fire.

I really wanted to go out on the deck for some heavy thinking. But the wind was still howling and the snow still flying.

"You ever been in love?" I asked.

"Been in *like* plenty of times."

I peered over at him.

"Never in love," he admitted.

"Same here. I wonder how you know when you're in love."

"You just know."

I chuckled. There were those two little

words—*just know*. But for some reason, they didn't irritate me.

"I've got something for you," Joe said quietly.

And I thought here it is, here comes the kiss. But I was wrong. I watched him stretch out and grab his duffle bag that he kept beside the recliner. Poor guy didn't even have a place to keep his clothes. How much more hospitable could my brother and I be?

"There's some empty drawers in the dresser in my bedroom," I said. "Why don't you put your things in there tomorrow?"

"Okay. Thanks."

"It's no big deal. You're using that bathroom to get ready in the morning. Might as well hang your stuff in my closet, too."

"Okay."

He unzipped a side pouch, removed a bag that I recognized, the bag he'd been holding the first day at A Novel Place. He pulled out a bookmark and handed it to me.

It was clear, a tiny purple and white flower pressed inside.

"I saw that and thought that since you like to read, maybe you'd like to have it. Then I chickened out of giving it to you, because I thought that since you like to read, you probably have a hundred bookmarks—"

"No," I said, cutting him off, thinking how sweet he was. "I don't have any bookmarks. I'm always using whatever scrap of paper is handy when I stop reading. This is beautiful. Thank you." I rose up on my knees, leaned toward him, and kissed him briefly on the lips. "I have to go to bed now."

I got up, clutching the bookmark to my chest like it was an entire bouquet of roses. "Thanks, again."

I hurried into my bedroom. Just as I'd surmised, Aunt Sue was sitting up in bed reading.

"Thought you were tired," I said. "Thought you were going to bed."

"Changed my mind."

I went to the nightstand, picked up my book, took out the grocery receipt that I was using to mark my place, and slipped the beautiful bookmark inside. Then I went into the bathroom and got ready for bed. When I came out, the lights were turned off.

I climbed into bed and lay there staring into the darkness.

"Aunt Sue?" I finally whispered.

"Yes, hon?"

"How many times have you been in love?"

"Just once."

"How did you know?"

"I just knew."

Great. What kind of answer was that from an experienced person?

"Were you scared?"

"Terrified."

Wonderful. Because the feelings I was starting to have for Joe were certainly bordering on terrifying. Definitely stronger than what I'd felt for Brad. Almost overwhelming.

"Sweet dreams," Aunt Sue said.

Yeah, right. To dream, you had to sleep.

I had a feeling thoughts of Joe were going to keep me awake the rest of the night.

# Chapter 18

"*We* have to stop meeting like this."

These were Aunt Sue's words to me as I came into A Novel Place just as the sun was starting to show itself. Even as I took a stool at the counter, she placed my mug of morning mint chocolate in front of me—already warmed, like she'd been expecting me.

The paper was spread out before her. But this morning she was working on a crossword puzzle, not reading ads.

The week had progressed nicely. I hardly ever thought about Brad anymore, mostly because I never saw him. I was spending more time on the slopes with Joe. Our relationship hadn't moved beyond friendship, but something there always seemed to be waiting.

I couldn't explain it.

Since the night of the storm, it seemed like I was seeing less of my friends. Leah was busy with her private lessons and Ian. I think the private lessons had been moved off the slopes to his apartment. She seldom had supper with us. Allie and Sam were always hanging out together at the Avalanche or a movie or who knew where. I'd tried spending my evenings with Aunt Sue, but I always started to feel guilty that we'd abandoned Joe, so eventually I would invite him over.

I mean, *Law and Order* reruns can only entertain you for so long.

He and Aunt Sue got along really well. We'd play poker, usually Texas Hold'em. I was always the first to lose all my chips. Aunt Sue and Joe would duke it out. Some nights one would take the pot, some nights the other would. The Kate-have-a-good-time fund had dwindled down to pennies.

The night before, Joe and I had finished searching every nook, cranny, shelf, wall, and door of the bookstore for Michael. We'd thought about giving it one more shot but patience wasn't my strong suit. So I'd decided this morning was *the* morning that I got the answer from Aunt Sue.

"Tell me about Michael," I demanded. "Joe said there's a picture of him hanging in the store. Which one is it?"

"Now, Kate, where's the fun in telling you? Besides, if I tell you, what will you and Joe do in the afternoons after you come down off the slopes?"

"We'll think of something. Come on. Tell me."

"But I like seeing you and Joe together."

I knew it. She'd probably never been serious about anyone named Michael. She was simply playing matchmaker.

"We've been skiing together," I assured her. "And we played poker at your place last night."

She peered at me. "Joe and I played poker. Your chips were gone in fifteen minutes."

"So I don't have a poker face."

"No, you don't. You never did. I can always tell exactly what you're thinking, and I think everyone else can, too."

"Everyone except Brad," I stated.

She gave me a pointed look.

I held up my hand. "I'm totally over him, so I don't need you playing matchmaker. Now where is Michael's photo?"

"It's in my office."

I stared at her, unable to believe that she'd given in so easily. "In your office? You told Joe that it was hanging on a wall in the store."

"My office is in the store."

"Not really."

I hopped off the stool, started toward the end of the counter, stopped, and gazed back at her. She was standing there, just watching me.

"Is it okay if I look?" I asked.

"Sure."

I thought about calling Joe. I had my cell phone in the zippered pocket of my jacket, but for some reason I didn't want to share this moment. All these years and Aunt Sue had never told me about this guy.

I went around the counter and through the door that led into her office. Even though I'd been there a hundred times before, I'd forgotten that there were like a thousand pictures on the walls. Okay, not a thousand, but at least two dozen.

These were different from the ones in the main area of the store, though.

These were pictures of Aunt Sue with my mom. Aunt Sue with me. Aunt Sue with Sam. Aunt Sue with both of us. Aunt Sue with my grandparents. Aunt Sue with . . .

Oh, my gosh. This had to be Michael. Aunt Sue was young. And so was he.

She was nestled up against his side. Both of them with broad smiles on their faces. In ski jackets with the mountains in the background. Here. At Snow Angel Valley.

I heard a quiet sound. I turned to find Aunt Sue standing there, looking at the picture that I was looking at. A wistful expression on her face. And I knew.

"He's dead, isn't he?" I said quietly. "That's the reason you didn't marry him."

She nodded.

"How?" I asked.

"We were college seniors. We came here for winter break. With some friends. He and another guy decided to be adventuresome, do some off-trail skiing. There was an avalanche."

"I'm so sorry, Aunt Sue—"

"It was a long time ago, Kate."

"Still, I'm sorry, and I'm sorry that I insisted you tell me about him. That I didn't respect your right to have your secrets."

She moved up and put her arm around me. "He was never a secret, but sometimes it's hard to tell people about him."

"How could you stay here?"

"How could I leave? Do you know, Katie, that on cold winter nights I can still hear his laughter coming down off the mountains? We loved it here. He once told me that he didn't want to die while sitting in front of the TV. He wanted a life of adventure. He wanted to go to novel places."

*A Novel Place.*

"Is that the reason you travel the world?" I asked.

"I travel the world because there is so much to see, so much to experience. And because I don't want to die sitting in front of a TV, either."

I hugged her tightly. "I love you, Aunt Sue."

"I love you, too, sweetie."

She wiped the tear from my cheek. "No tears now, Katie. I've had other guys in my life, just none like Michael. The important thing is for you to go out and enjoy life. Get cozy with a ski instructor or Sam's friend. Don't wait for life to tap you on the shoulder. Go out and tap *it*."

Tap life on the shoulder. Aunt Sue made it sound so easy. I didn't think I was doing a terrible job of it. Okay, I had hid out for a while and moped about Brad. But I was over that. I was making progress. Today I wanted to go to the top of Devil's Peak and shout at the top of my lungs.

When we arrived at the ski resort, we did our usual pairing: Leah off to take her private lessons, Allie and Sam off to do their thing, Joe and I to take the ski lift to the slopes.

It was a long journey to the top.

"You're awfully quiet this morning," he finally said. "You okay?"

Was I? I thought so. I was amazed, though, that he always seemed so good at reading me. I suppose I shouldn't have been, no poker face and all that, but still he seemed to better than most.

"Just distracted," I admitted.

"Anything I can help you with?"

I looked over at him. At his serious eyes. The way he was studying me with true concern.

Joe and I were friends. Which I was beginning to think was the only thing I was going to find this winter break. Friendship.

Not a bad thing, I guessed. Unless you're hankering for more.

"I found out about Michael," I said quietly. I took a deep breath. "He was killed in an avalanche. Right here at Snow Angel Valley. When Aunt Sue was really young."

"Geez. Total bummer."

"I know. I feel badly that I insisted she tell me, even though she says she's okay with it."

"Kate, you shouldn't feel bad. She must have wanted you to know or she never would have brought him up to begin with. I mean, she was the one who first mentioned him, right?"

I nodded.

"So she was ready to tell you about him."

"I guess so." I couldn't even begin to imagine Brad trying to console me like that.

"I can't believe your aunt never found anyone else."

How typical of a guy to think love was just about moving on. I'd read somewhere once that when a man lost his wife, he looked for a replacement. When a woman lost her husband, she looked for love again. It was that whole men are from Mars thing. They just so don't get it.

"I don't think she wanted to find a replacement for him."

He grimaced. "I didn't mean to sound insensitive. I just mean she's totally cool. I would have thought any number of guys would have been interested in her."

"She's dated a lot. I've even met some of the guys. And she always seemed to have a good time with them. But I guess she wants more than that in marriage. I don't know. I guess for it to really work, the intensity of the feelings have to go both ways, you know?"

It seemed like at that minute he was trying to search deep into my soul.

"Yeah, I know." He looked forward. "Get ready."

I hadn't realized that we'd already arrived at the drop-off point. Even though it seemed like

I'd done this a hundred times, I always felt this little adrenaline rush when I shoved myself off the seat and landed on the small slope leading away from lift. I had to be quick so the chair didn't knock me down and I had to get out of the way so the next person in line could disembark.

Deep breath—

And I was off, skiing down the slight incline, always amazed that I didn't fall on my butt or make a fool of myself. That little thrill of self-accomplishment.

Joe was beside me, all the way down the short run.

Then we made our way to the line at Devil's Peak, waiting our turn to go down the awesome trail. I could see the tree line. Devil's Peak led to various tree-lined trails, with many turns, lots of powder. The line of people moved quickly, because you didn't have to wait for the person in front of you to reach the bottom.

You just kinda took your bearings, then you were off.

"Meet you at the bottom," I said to Joe. Then I shoved off.

Skiing is a real trip. It's about freedom and speed.

But it can also be dangerous because of the speed, the unforeseen terrain. Actors, politicians, sons of politicians. They all make the news when they have a skiing accident. You have to stay focused.

I wasn't focused.

I was thinking about Aunt Sue and Michael. I was thinking about loving someone that much. I was thinking about living life to the fullest. I was thinking about Joe. I was thinking about the kiss he gave me, the kiss he almost gave me. I was wondering why I was afraid of letting myself go with him, of letting him know that I was beginning to think of him as more than a friend. I was thinking about everything except what I was doing.

So once I was down past the tree line onto the narrower trail, I took the first curve a little faster than I should have, lost my balance —

Struggled to slow down, to remain upright —

Lost the battle.

Hit the ground hard. Slid a few feet before coming to a stop.

Heard a yell.

Saw a flash of movement.

Watched as a skier tumbled past me.

His momentum carried him farther.

The trees stopped him.

He just lay there.

Not moving.

My heart leaped into my throat. My chest tightened painfully. I couldn't breathe.

I stared at the fallen skier and all I could think was *No! No! No!*

It was Joe.

# Chapter 19

"*I* can't believe Joe had a skiing accident," Sam said, shaking his head, sitting beside me in the waiting room of the emergency clinic in Snow Angel Valley. He didn't sound disgusted. Simply stunned.

I'd never been as scared in my life as I was when I'd made my way over to Joe, sprawled beneath that tree. It had seemed to take forever for Joe to sit up and reassure me that he was fine.

"A little bruised maybe, but nothing serious." He'd even chuckled.

But when he'd tried to stand, it was obvious that he wasn't fine. His leg couldn't bear any weight and it buckled beneath him. He'd even cursed harshly when he'd reached out to a tree for support.

"Here, lean on me," I'd said.

"I'm too heavy for you."

"I'll call the first-aid station."

"It's not that bad. I can make it down the slope. But, I need you to carry my skis."

He'd tried hopping, stopping occasionally to lean against a tree and rest.

Someone must have seen us struggling to get him down the mountain, because eventually the mountain rescue team paramedics had arrived. They were dressed in red so they were clearly visible. When they'd put Joe on a stretcher, I'd felt sick to my stomach that I hadn't gone with my gut instinct and called them.

Guys can be so stubborn, always trying to appear so macho. Asking for directions or help simply isn't in their genetic makeup.

Then I pulled my cell phone from my jacket pocket and called Sam. He and Allie met us at the first-aid station. Although Joe couldn't walk, his leg didn't seem to be broken, and he'd assured the medics that he didn't need to be transported in an ambulance.

So Sam had driven him to the emergency clinic.

"I finally get to ride shotgun," Joe had quipped from the front seat, his face ashen.

How could he crack jokes? Didn't he realize how serious this was? How guilty I felt or how worried I was?

Allie and I had been in the back. It wasn't until we got to the clinic that I remembered Leah. Right now, Allie was outside talking to her on her cell phone, letting her know what had happened, where we were, and what our immediate plans were. Not that any of us really knew. We only knew that cell phones weren't allowed in the emergency clinic. Their frequency signals affected heart monitors or something, which we figured out when the Nurse Ratchet doppelganger at the admittance desk gave Allie a stern look when she'd taken out her cell phone. Allie had actually gone pale. That look had sent her scurrying out the door to make the call.

Joe was off in an examination room somewhere. And I was sitting here with my brother, wondering if I should confess that it was my fault because I hadn't been paying attention to what I was doing on the slopes. But confessing would result in a dressing down. I really wasn't in the mood to have my brother chew me out.

"It happened so fast," I said, wondering if I sounded as guilty as I felt.

"People forget how dangerous skiing can be. It's like driving a car. You have to pay attention all the time."

"Yeah," I replied, the single word strangled.

"Joe's always so focused, I figured he was the last one who'd get distracted. I mean the guy finished the semester with a four-point-oh."

I looked over at Sam.

He shrugged. "All A's."

"What were your grades?" I asked, looking for something to distract me from my worries.

"I'm not telling."

This was the most secretive winter break I'd ever had. Even I was keeping secrets now.

Sam reached over and put his arm around me, squeezing me close, one buddy to another. "It wasn't your fault, Kate. Don't worry, he'll be fine."

Only he didn't look too fine when he finally hobbled out on crutches.

"Wrenched my knee," he said, wincing.

"Bummer, dude," Sam said.

Could Sam get any more unsympathetic? Had to be a guy thing.

"Does it hurt?" I asked stupidly.

"Like a bitch, but the doc gave me some pain medicine samples to get me through until I can get the prescription filled."

In one of the hands clutching a crutch was dangling a white slip of paper. I snatched it away. "I'll get this filled for you."

"Thanks."

He looked over at Sam. "Sorry to have messed up your day."

"Sorry you messed up your knee."

"Look, if you can just get me to the condo, I'll be fine. Then you can get back out on the slopes."

"We're not going back out on the slopes," I said.

"Course you are. No sense in everyone's fun being ruined. Set me up on the couch in front of the TV and I'll be fine."

Funny thing was, maybe he thought he was going to be fine, but I wasn't so sure about myself. I kept having this irrational urge to cry.

Just our luck, we couldn't find any *Law and Order* reruns, so on my way back from the pharmacy, I stopped by the Movies-4-Less video store and picked up the first three seasons of *24* plus a couple of seasons of *Buffy*.

I also stopped by A Novel Place to let Aunt Sue know what had happened.

"I'll bring over some special hot chocolate this evening," she said.

"That would be great."

By the time I got back to the condo, Sam, my oh-so-sensitive brother, and his equally sensitive girlfriend had headed back to the slopes. Sam going didn't surprise me, but I'd expected Allie to stay and help me take care of Joe, even though Joe insisted that I catch the shuttle back to the slopes and join them. A shuttle ran every half hour from the village to the mountains. I wasn't a big fan of shuttle buses, but more than that, I wasn't a big fan of deserting someone in pain, especially when I was responsible for that pain.

"Look, really, I'm going to be fine," Joe said. "Go have fun. We have less than two weeks left; then we're back to the real world of textbooks, essays, and exams."

He was sitting back in the recliner, his foot propped up on a pillow to keep his leg elevated to reduce the swelling, a bag of ice on top of his knee, a sleepy look on his face. I guessed that Allie had taken care of getting his leg situated and the pain medicine the doctor gave him was kicking in.

"I'm not going to go have fun. I'm going to fix you some lunch."

"Don't do that." He was practically whining, which was so unlike Joe. He always gave the appearance of being so tough. "I won't be able to follow the rules. I won't be able to clean the kitchen. I'll get kicked out of the condo. I'll have to sleep in the snow."

I stared at him. "You're kidding, right? You don't really think I'm going to make you clean the kitchen."

"But the rules—"

"Forget the rules."

He gave me this goofy grin that seemed to say, "Lighten up, Kate." Yep, the pain medicine was starting to work.

"In that case"—he waved his arm—"have at it. I'll have double what you're having and some hot apple cider."

I made us tuna fish–on-toast sandwiches. I set the plate in his lap and a bowl of chips on the table beside him, along with the hot cinnamon apple cider. Then I sat on the couch and nibbled on my own sandwich, but my mouth was dry, my throat thick.

On the TV, Jack Bauer was in deep trouble. Again.

"I think this is the best sandwich I've ever eaten," Joe said.

I glanced over at him. "Do you want another one?"

"Nah, this'll do me." He was studying me. "You don't have to wait on me, Kate."

"I want to."

"Why?"

I set my sandwich aside. I thought it was the worst I'd ever eaten. Probably because I kept feeling like I was going to choke on it. My throat felt thick. And I was having a difficult time swallowing.

"It was my fault you got hurt."

"It wasn't your fault."

"I lost my balance and skidded first."

"Okay, I guess that makes you the winner then."

"This isn't about winning."

"It's not about blame, either. Look, I screwed up. It's no big deal. I'll be fine in a few days. So go back to the mountain."

"I don't want to go to the mountain." I came to my feet. "How many times do I have to say it? I don't want to go because—"

I stopped abruptly, biting back what I was about to say. I didn't want to go back to the mountain because Joe wasn't going to be there. And without Joe, where was the fun?

No, it was more than the fun. It was something else, something I couldn't quite describe. It was that frightening sensation that kept me awake at nights. The thought that Joe might mean a lot more to me than I was ready for.

Only I couldn't tell him all that. Didn't want to tell him all that. I'd made a fool of myself over Brad, and for all I knew, Joe had been keeping me company out of pity. He was with me because there was no one else.

"Because why?" he asked.

I snatched up his empty plate, grabbed mine. "I owe you," I said. "Because it *was* my fault and you'll never convince me that it wasn't."

I marched to the kitchen, dumped my sandwich down the disposal, and put the plates in the dishwasher. Then I did something really stupid.

I cried.

Cried because my heart had leaped into my throat when I'd seen him tumbling down the slope toward the trees, cried because I'd been terrified, cried because somehow I'd really started to care for him.

Cried because he didn't want me around.

I grabbed a dishtowel and wiped my tears. The last was just tough.

I was going to take care of Joe whether he wanted me to or not. I was going to take care of him until he was better.

Whether he wanted it or not.

I'd made up my mind. Nothing was going to make me change it.

# Chapter 20

$O$kay. I was a lousy Florence Nightingale.

"I should take your temperature," I suggested, standing between Joe and the TV with a thermometer in my hand. I'd found a first-aid kit beneath the sink in the bathroom. It contained little plastic covers to put over the thermometer to make it sanitary.

Joe was not impressed. He shook his head. "I don't have the flu. I have a banged-up knee."

"What if it gets infected? One of the first signs would be running a fever, and if it gets infected—"

"It's not going to get infected."

"How do you know?"

"I just know."

I returned the thermometer to the first-aid

kit and put it back in the cabinet.

"I should make you some chicken soup," I announced when I returned to the living room.

"I don't want chicken soup. I don't have a cold."

I tapped my foot and studied him. I felt absolutely useless. "I'll get you some more ice for your leg."

Before he could protest, I took the blue bag that the doctor had given him and dumped the icy water that was more ice than water. Okay, maybe I'd gone for changing the ice bag a bit too soon. I put in fresh ice, carried it back to the living room, and gently placed it over his bandage-wrapped knee.

"Kate, there's really nothing for you to do. You should head back to the slopes."

I curled up on one end of the couch. "I'm not going to leave you alone."

"I'm a big boy. I can take care of myself."

"Look, by the time I catch the shuttle and get back to the mountain, it'll almost be time to turn around and come back home. It's too much energy."

And I'd be alone. I had no interest in being alone.

"I guess you're right. Tomorrow, though, you go out with Sam."

"We'll see."

I was tired of battling. Tomorrow I'd be refreshed and could start anew. Because I wasn't going to leave him alone. No matter what he said.

He yawned. "The medicine is making me drowsy. I'm going to take a nap."

"Okay." I took the afghan that was lying across the back of the couch and draped it over him.

"Can I get you anything?" I asked.

He slowly shook his head. "Nope."

His eyes drifted closed.

"Are you comfortable?" I asked.

"Except for the throbbing ache in my knee, I'm fine."

A pang of guilt hit me.

He opened his eyes. "I didn't even think to ask how you were."

"Me? I'm fine."

"You took a spill, too."

"I bruised my hip a little, but that's all."

"We were both really lucky," he said.

He closed his eyes.

We were lucky. I knew that. And it was sweet that he'd asked about me. The bruise on my hip was going to be about the size of an orange, but at least I was mobile.

"Should I turn off the TV?" I asked.

"Nah, you can watch it. The sound won't bother me."

"But I rented the DVDs for you to watch."

He opened his eyes again. "Thanks, I'll watch them later."

"They didn't have any *Law and Order* DVDs or I would have gotten those."

"What you got is great."

"What's your favorite meal? I'll make it for supper."

"Kate—"

"We'll have a party here tonight, so you're not alone."

"I don't mind being alone."

"I can go to A Novel Place—"

"Do that."

"—and get you some books to read. What

do you like to read?"

"Science fiction."

"I don't know much about science fiction."

"Go talk with Paige."

I looked at the door, looked back at Joe. He'd closed his eyes again. His breathing was even.

I crept over to the couch, sat down, and watched him.

It should have been boring. Like watching a rock or something.

But Joe wasn't boring. Not even when he was sleeping. I realized that I'd pretty much been bugging him, making a nuisance of myself. Worrying about him.

And the worrying about him had *me* worried.

When had I started liking him so much? When had he become my friend as much as he was Sam's? Maybe more so.

Why hadn't he tried to kiss me again?

Did I want him to kiss me again? Did I want him to make another deposit in the Kate-have-a-good-time fund?

Sitting there watching him, thinking about it, I decided that, yeah, I did.

❖ ❖ ❖

Joe received an incredible amount of attention when everyone got home that evening. Since Leah hadn't seen him since his accident, she made him describe his plummet down the slope in gory detail. I held my breath, waiting for the moment when he revealed that it had been my fault, but he never did. It added to my guilt. I didn't want to call him a liar, but leaving out my part left him vulnerable, because Sam, in typical Sam fashion, was razzing Joe about being a klutz. Joe took it all with good humor. He was really something.

Allie was doing the things that I'd been doing: getting him something to drink, swapping out DVDs.

Aunt Sue and Paige came over. Aunt Sue I'd expected. Paige was a surprise. I didn't like seeing the way she coddled Joe, making him laugh with her exaggerated care, putting a pillow behind his head, rubbing his shoulders, offering to give him a bath.

A bath. I wanted to gag.

And I really liked Paige, so being irritated with her was a little unsettling. I wasn't jealous. Was I?

Then Brad and Cynthia arrived. Had someone broadcast an announcement on the local news station?

I was in the kitchen chopping up chicken for a chicken spaghetti casserole. Casseroles were one-dish wonders. Made great leftovers. And I decided that thinking about all the benefits of casseroles was a lot better than thinking about Paige flirting with poor Joe.

Allie was putting together a salad. Leah was mixing up some brownies. It was the brownies that the guys would ooh and aah over. Not that I cared if my efforts were barely appreciated.

I mean, Joe hadn't bothered to thank me once for all I'd done for him that afternoon. And he was a lousy patient. Most guys are from what I understand. But he became the worst after he woke up from his nap, like he was trying to drive me away.

Adjust the afghan, bring me some water, bring me some juice, hot chocolate, hot apple cider, turn up the TV, turn it down, change the DVD. Honestly, you'd think he was completely helpless.

Okay, so he was pretty helpless. I'd actually

spent some time in my bedroom moving around using only one leg, trying to raise my sympathy level when I got really frustrated with him. I couldn't complain about his demanding attitude because he *had* told me not to hang around. So my unhappiness with him was totally my fault. I didn't like that, either.

"Geez, are you trying to murder that chicken?" Leah asked.

I looked at the cutting board. The chopped chicken was pretty much annihilated.

"I like it finely chopped," I said.

"Yeah, well, it's finely chopped."

I scooped it into the casserole dish where spaghetti noodles, cheese, and peas were already waiting.

"Want me to chase Cynthia and Brad away?" she asked.

I shook my head. "I don't care that they're here."

She arched an eyebrow. "Really? You're totally over Brad?"

"Totally."

"That's great! Ian has a friend—"

"No thanks."

"But he's another Aussie ski instructor and—"

"Doesn't matter. I'll be busy taking care of Joe."

Leah looked at me, her eyes blinking. "He's not helpless, you know."

"Not completely, no. But he can't get around very easily. And he's definitely not going to be able to go to the slopes. I can't just leave him here alone to fend for himself."

She narrowed her eyes. "Why not?"

"Because she likes him too much," Allie said.

I jerked my attention to her.

She shrugged. "Don't you?"

I sorta felt like I was playing revolving door crush, leapfrogging from liking one of my brother's friends to the other. I mean, that should have been a strike against Joe: hanging out with my brother.

Of course, now one of my best friends was hanging *all over* my brother. . . .

"I don't know what I feel," I admitted. "I mean, I like him, sure. He's nice. And okay, I feel responsible for his present condition. I fell first. He fell trying not to run over me."

"So you're going to spend time with him out of obligation?"

"I'm going to spend time with him because he needs me."

I wasn't about to admit that maybe I needed him, too.

# Chapter 21

$A$s the days went by, Joe became the worst patient on the planet.

He didn't like being waited on, didn't want people canceling their plans because of him. I offered him my bed because he couldn't get down the stairs to sleep in the bed that Brad had vacated. I'd magnanimously offered to sleep in Brad's bed and share the room with my brother. But I guess Joe figured out what a great sacrifice the offer was on my part, because he said that he was fine still sleeping on the couch or in the recliner.

The first night I started out checking on him every hour on the hour—in case he needed pain medicine or something to drink or eat, or a DVD changed in the player.

The answer was always the same: I don't need anything, Kate.

Eventually I gave up and stretched out on the couch so he could call for me if he needed anything. He slept in the recliner.

He never did wake me up to get him anything. But a couple of times I woke up and found him staring at me. He always looked guilty for doing it, like maybe he shouldn't be watching me sleep. The thing was: I lost track of how much I watched him sleep. I just liked looking at him.

The third day we were both snappish. Lack of good sleep and guilt were responsible for my bad mood. I think Joe simply wasn't used to being housebound.

He was hobbling around the living room.

"You need to use your crutches," I chastised him.

"I need to get out of here."

"Yeah, well, you can't get out of here. You're injured."

"I can't ski, but I'm moving around better. I could go outside and build a snowman."

"How are you going to get to the backyard

where the snow is? There are stairs, you know."

"I can hop down or scoot down on my butt."

I shook my head. "I don't think that's a good idea."

He studied me hard. "Okay. How 'bout the hot tub?"

"What about it?"

"I think the swirling hot water would be good for my knee, and there are no steps leading to it. Should be a breeze getting to it."

"There's the freezing-our-butts-getting-in-and-out factor to consider." Besides, did I really want to be in a small tub with him, especially since I had no bathing suit? I mean, who brings a bathing suit to a ski resort?

"Snowman it is then," he said.

*Stubborn, obstinate, crazy* were words that flittered through my mind as I watched him struggle into his jacket, standing on one leg, before reaching down for his crutches.

"You coming?" he asked.

I stared at him. "You can't be serious about going out there."

"Dead serious. With or without you. Although without you, I could trip and freeze to death before anyone found me."

That wasn't likely to happen. He was just being difficult. On the other hand, I was going a little stir crazy as well.

"Yeah, I'll come."

I put on my own jacket, jerked my knitted cap down over my ears, and stuffed my hair up beneath it. I wanted to be there when he realized that getting down wasn't hard . . . but getting back up the stairs?

That was going to be a different story.

It's a little difficult to build an awesome snowman when your mobility is limited.

Joe made it down the stairs by gripping the rail and hopping from one step to the next, holding both crutches in one hand. Once he got to the ground, he went only a couple of feet. The crutches were sinking into the foot of snow that covered the backyard. Eventually, Joe gave up and dropped to the ground.

It took willpower on my part not to rush to his aid.

"Okay, so crutches on snow don't work so well," he said, peering up at me as I stood on the steps looking down on him.

I worked really hard not to gloat. "Tried to tell you."

"Well, I'm here now. I might as well enjoy it."

But he sure didn't sound like he was on the verge of enjoying it.

I moved nimbly down the stairs and knelt in the snow beside him. "What now, genius?"

Okay, so I was gloating a little bit.

He scooped up some snow, packed it into a ball, and held it up. "I make little snowmen."

What he actually did, after packing snow around his knee, was make a little snowman village. Kinda like what I created when I went to the beach and made sand castles.

Only he made a little igloo house and had small snowmen standing around it. I'd actually gone into the house and brought out some little hard-shelled candies that he used for the eyes. He was partial to using the green pieces. So here were all these snowmen with eyes like mine.

"You're pretty good," I said.

"It's not the first time that I've hurt myself while I was skiing. I've broken my leg twice, so

I learned pretty quickly to look for other entertainment." He tapped his snow covered knee. "This is a walk in the park."

"More like a hop in the park," I corrected him.

He grinned. "Yeah. More like that."

"Did the doctor say how long you'd have to use the crutches?" I asked.

"He told me to use them until I got home, then have my doctor check out the knee."

He gathered up more snow, mashed it together. "You know, Kate, this wasn't your fault."

Those words had become his mantra over the past few days. I was really growing tired of them.

"I know that. I tried to talk you out of coming out here."

He peered over at me. "Not me sitting in the snow. My busted knee. It wasn't your fault. You shouldn't feel like you have to stay with me and pay penance."

"I don't feel that way."

He lobbed the snowball at me.

"Hey!"

"Come on, Kate. Admit it. You're only here because you feel guilty." He shoveled more snow at me.

"Cut it out!"

He threw more snow at me. "Make me!"

"Stop it! You're gonna hurt yourself."

"What if I do?"

"Then I'll be stuck taking care of you longer."

The snow stopped flying. He'd destroyed his village and all his snowmen.

Joe was breathing heavily. So was I. But there was something in his eyes, kinda like that first night when he mentioned that he'd seen me when I went to visit Sam.

Disappointment, embarrassment. Something else.

"I don't want you here out of obligation, Kate." He started scooting toward the steps.

"Here, I'll help you."

"I don't want your help," he ground out.

I stood helplessly while he made his way to the steps, dragging his crutches behind him. He sat on the bottom step, put his hands behind him and pulled himself up to the next step.

"Joe—"

"Go have some fun, Kate."

"Joe—"

"I mean it, Kate. Get the hell out of here!"

The anger in his voice hurt. I'd been trying so hard to take good care of him, and he wasn't appreciating it at all.

"Okay, fine, I will."

"Good."

"Great!"

Without looking back, I trudged toward the street. I didn't know where I was going to go. I just knew where I didn't want to be.

Anywhere near Joe.

"Hiding away?"

I peered up from the mystery novel I was reading to find Aunt Sue looking down on me. It was the middle of the afternoon. Everyone was on the slopes, no customers in the shop. I'd made myself some hot mint chocolate, located a book with a lot of murder and mayhem, curled up on a loveseat near the fireplace, and was happily envisioning Joe as the corpse of this tale.

"If I was hiding away, I wouldn't do it in your store where you'd be sure to find me," I said.

She'd been in her office when I arrived, and I hadn't bothered to poke my head inside to say hello. So maybe I was hiding from her a little, even though I was in plain sight.

She sat down on the loveseat across from me. "You should find something to do that's more fun than reading a book in my store."

"Strange words from a bookseller. Your profit is dependent upon people thinking that reading is fun."

"Kate, really, what's wrong?"

"Nothing is wrong."

"Then why are you hiding out?"

"I'm not hiding out. You found me, didn't you? And you didn't even have to look."

"I didn't say you were hiding from me. You're hiding from Joe."

Did she have to be so good at figuring me out all the time? It was really irritating.

"He kicked me out, okay?"

"How can a guy who only has one good leg to stand on kick you out?"

I knew she was trying to be funny, but her

words hurt, because I had to face the truth. I felt the tears burn the back of my eyes. "He doesn't want me around."

"I find that hard to believe, Katie."

"Yeah, well, he threw snow at me and told me to leave."

She looked astounded. As well she should be.

"Where did he get snow?" she asked.

Okay, I'd obviously misread the reason for her astonishment. It wasn't that he'd thrown snow *at* me, but that he'd *had* snow to throw.

"He went outside to build a snowman."

"A snowman? Outside? How did he manage that? His knee must be getting better."

"Not really. He hopped down the steps." I bobbed my head from side to side, deciding whether or not to spill it all. "He wanted to go in the hot tub, but I said no, so he decided to go build a snowman. He said he was tired of being cooped up."

"You should have picked Door Number One. The hot tub. Way more fun."

"Aunt Sue, be serious. I've really started to like him, and it's so hard because I'm a terrible nurse."

"Doesn't sound to me like he's looking for a nurse. Besides, knowing men like I do, he's probably a lousy patient."

"Understatement."

"He's been locked in for three days. He's probably ready to get out of there."

"Another understatement. But he can't go skiing."

"There's other things to do."

"Like what?"

"Hot tub."

I glared at her. She smiled.

"Don't knock it until you've tried it."

"Well, I saw Cynthia and Brad try it and she got the sniffles. That's the last thing either Joe or I need. Something else to keep us condo-bound."

"So take some time away from him and go skiing tomorrow. He probably feels guilty for ruining your fun."

And I felt guilty for ruining his. Plus the truth was, I'd discovered that I didn't want to be away from him. Just staying here at the store instead of going back to the condo was really hard. Punishing him with my absence was punishment for me as well.

Aunt Sue stood and winked at me. "Honestly, Kate, give him what he asked for: a day without you around. Haven't you ever heard that absence makes the heart grow fonder?"

Yeah, I'd heard that, but it was another one of her sayings that just didn't seem to make a whole lot of sense.

I watched her walk away. Maybe I was a little afraid that he'd decide he liked me being absent. Maybe that was the problem. I was afraid that my absence wouldn't make his heart grow fonder. Instead he'd just forget about me if I wasn't completely in his face.

The door to the shop opened and Leah walked in. She wasn't in her ski clothes. Just jeans, a sweater, and a jacket.

"Hey! Joe told me that he thought I'd find you here."

It was a little scary how well Joe knew me. I hadn't told him where I was going. Granted the options were limited, but still, I hated the thought of being so predictable. Predictable was boring, right?

Leah dropped down on the love seat that Aunt Sue had just vacated.

"You're in early from the slopes," I said.

"Yeah. Ian needed to teach a class, so I thought I'd come into town and take care of a few things."

"Doesn't he teach class every day?"

"Yeah, but only for a few hours. Sometimes I hang around with the class, sometimes I ski, sometimes I just wait for him at the restaurant. Today I decided to do something."

"Want some hot chocolate?"

"No, I'm cool. I needed to talk to you."

She sounded serious. I thought of Sam on the slopes—

"What's wrong? Did something happen to Sam? To Allie? Are they hurt?"

She held up a hand. "Oh, no, it's nothing bad. Sorry, I wasn't thinking. But I swear it's nothing bad."

I felt my heartbeat return to normal, and knew I'd overreacted. I mean, if it had been anything really serious, she would have begun with it, not told me about how she spent time with Ian.

"What is it then?" I asked.

She scrunched up her face. I could see this was really hard for her.

"You're starting to scare me again, Leah."

"Okay. I'm sorry. It's just that, well, I'm gonna pull a Brad on you."

"You're going to start totally ignoring me?"

She smiled, then grimaced. "I'm going to move out of the condo."

"Why would you do that? Where are you going to go?"

"I'm going to go stay with Ian. I want to be with him as much as possible before winter break ends."

"Well, this is a surprise."

She bobbed her head. "I've totally fallen for him. Really bad. I don't know how I'm going to go back to Texas, Kate."

"On an airplane."

She scowled at me. "I'm serious here. I don't want to leave him."

Wow! That happened fast. I was stunned.

"You've got another semester of high school before you graduate."

"I know. And my parents would kill me if I

didn't come home. And besides, I want to finish high school with my friends, go through graduation and all that with you and Allie. But after I graduate . . . I think I'm coming back here to live."

"You said a ski instructor was supposed to be temporary."

"Well, he was supposed to be, and I thought he would be, but the truth is, I'm crazy about him."

I didn't know what to say, except the truth. "I'm happy for you, Leah."

"I'm happy for me, too." She scooted up. "Listen, I know you have the bedroom with the king-size bed and sleeping on a bunk bed isn't glamorous, but with me leaving and Joe unable to navigate stairs—"

"I could move down to your room, and he wouldn't have to sleep on the couch."

She nodded.

He hadn't gone for me bunking in with Sam, probably because he knew what a sacrifice it would be. But sharing a room with my best friend? No sweat. Allie and I had slept over at each other's houses too many times to count.

"Would I be sleeping in the top or bottom bunk?"

She shrugged. "Whichever one you wanted."

"Which one does Allie sleep in?"

She looked at the fire burning in the fireplace. "She doesn't exactly."

"What do you mean?"

"You know, the basement is kind of a world unto itself. A lot goes on that people don't realize is going on."

I finally got it. Allie and Sam . . . heavy duty secret handshaking going on.

"Oh," I said.

"Yeah."

I nodded. "Thanks for the offer to move downstairs, but I think I'll stay where I am. I don't need to be any closer to the action, if you know what I mean. It's probably best to let the secrets in the basement stay in the basement."

"Kinda like 'what happens in Vegas, stays in Vegas'?"

"Exactly. I think what happens in Snow Angel Valley needs to stay in Snow Angel Valley."

I was also wondering if Aunt Sue had another open condo that I could move into. How was it that with everyone moving out, the condo suddenly seemed way too crowded?

# Chapter 22

The next morning I was in the kitchen fixing French toast for breakfast. It was strange not having Leah here. Stranger still to know that I was going to go to the slopes for the day, maybe hook up with one of Ian's friends. She'd called me last night to see what I thought about the idea. I told her I'd call her when I got there.

I knew it would be fun. And I wasn't certain why I was so reluctant to commit. . . .

Okay, I was reluctant because I felt guilty about having any kind of fun at all. I knew I shouldn't. After all, Joe was insisting that I go. And Aunt Sue was probably right. Time away from each other was what we both needed.

We'd sorta made up after I came back to the

condo yesterday. Enough so that we shared supper, watched TV, and played a couple of games of checkers. Right now, Joe was in the shower.

"What are you making? I'm starving."

I spun around. Brad was standing in the doorway, wearing a T-shirt and jeans, his feet bare, his short hair somehow looking tousled. His face unshaven.

"What are you doing here?" I asked.

He rolled his shoulders into a big shrug. "Things with Cyn didn't work out. I moved back over here last night."

*That* was a surprise!

"Funny. Nobody mentioned it."

He rubbed his jaw. "It was pretty late when I knocked on the back door. Joe let me in."

"Oh." I didn't know what else to say. "Sorry about you and Cynthia."

He shrugged again. "It happens."

"So you want some breakfast?"

"Yeah, but you know what I want more?"

He walked into the kitchen until he was standing almost in front of me. "I'd like you to go skiing with me today."

I smiled. "Go skiing with you?"

"Yeah. Ever since that night on the deck, when you let me in to get my stuff, I haven't been able to stop thinking about you."

"Oh, yeah?"

Why did I suddenly feel triumphant, vindicated, sexier than Cynthia? Why did it seem that my Brad-ectomy was coming undone?

"Yeah."

He put his hands on my waist and grinned broadly.

"So how 'bout it? You and me on the slopes, babe. We'll have a great time."

Babe? No one had ever called me babe before. I thought it should have made me feel special. Funny that it didn't.

I caught movement out of the corner of my eye. I turned my head and saw Joe standing there balanced on his crutches, his hair still wet from the shower, watching us. I don't know what my face revealed but it couldn't have been good, because Joe looked like I'd just kicked his bad leg.

He spun around, started to move away.

"Joe, wait!"

I tried to go after him, but Brad was still holding me.

"Let me go," I ordered.

"Not until you say you'll go skiing with me."

"Hold this," I said holding up the bowl.

He got a confused look on his face before taking the bowl with both hands. With his hands no longer on my waist, I was able to slip away.

Much to my surprise, Joe, with his injured leg, had made it out to the deck already. He was standing at the railing looking out at the mountains by the time I caught up with him.

"Joe, let me explain."

"You don't have to explain, Kate," he said without looking at me, without emotion. "The reason you don't win at poker is because you don't have a poker face. Everything you're thinking and feeling is clearly written on your face."

"Apparently it isn't."

He turned then, his expression hard. "Go skiing with him, Kate."

"I don't want to go skiing with him."

"Yes, you do. And it's fine with me if you do. Because the truth is I was only hanging out with you because you were the only one left, and I felt sorry for you."

"That's a mean thing to say."

"It's the truth. You've wanted Brad from day one. Well, now you can have him."

"But what about you? Your knee?"

"I told you yesterday that I could take care of myself."

And he'd managed just fine without me, better than I'd managed without him. And Aunt Sue had convinced me that I needed a day away from Joe and that he needed a day away from me.

Why not spend the day with Brad? He was available, and apparently, so was I.

I nodded. "Great, then. I'm outta here."

Have you ever wanted something so badly, thought you'd die if you didn't get it, then when you finally did get it, you wondered what all the fuss was about?

I was sorta feeling that way as we drove to the slopes with Brad and me in the backseat, Sam and Allie in the front.

It was like Brad and I didn't have *anything* to talk about; we had absolutely nothing in common.

I mean, here he was, the guy of my dreams, and all I could think was: Why had I ever crushed on him to begin with?

And why was he suddenly so *not* hot?

He looked the same as he did the first time I saw him, and he *was* good looking. He did have a killer smile.

But I just couldn't seem to get excited about the fact that we were sorta having a date. I mean, he'd asked me to go skiing with him, and so here I was, and my heart should have been pounding.

But it wasn't.

I could have been going to the grocery store to pick up a bag of potatoes for all the thudding it was doing.

On top of that, an unnatural silence filled the car, like none of us could think of anything to say.

The weather, I finally thought. The weather was always a good topic of conversation.

"That was some blizzard we had last week, wasn't it?" I asked, since he'd been at Cynthia's instead of with us. We could talk about the blackouts, the shrieking winds—

He perked up, looked around. "There's a

Dairy Queen in town? I didn't know that. Where is it?"

I heard Allie snicker.

Sam took up for his friend. "It's an understandable mistake."

He looked in the rearview mirror. "She's talking about that storm that came through a few nights ago."

"Oh, bummer," Brad said. "I was craving an Oreo *Blizzard*."

We did a round of everyone naming off their favorite flavor of *Blizzard*. Then we were once again surrounded by awkward silence.

That was what really bugged me. How awkward it seemed not to be talking. I could sit with Joe for long stretches of time, not say a word, but never feel uncomfortable, never feel like the silence absolutely needed to be filled.

And here I was racking my brain for anything to talk about.

"No football games on TV tonight, right?" I said.

"Right," Sam said.

"Maybe we should rent some DVDs."

Brad ran his finger along my cheek. I wondered why it didn't send delicious shivers racing along my skin.

"I was thinking we'd go to the Avalanche," Brad said. "There's supposed to be a wicked awesome band starting tonight: The Abominable Snowmen."

I shrugged. "I don't know. I hate to leave Joe alone all day *and* all night."

"He's getting around better," Sam said. "I could drive him over to the Avalanche, so he could at least enjoy the band, be around people."

"You'd do that?" I asked.

"Sure. He's my friend. That's what friends do."

"That might make him feel better. It's gotta be hard, not being able to get out and do things."

"All right, then. We'll plan on going to the Avalanche tonight."

"Thanks."

"Why are you thanking me?"

Because he was doing something nice for Joe and that made it feel like he was doing something nice for me. But how did I explain that without sounding totally lame?

"Just because."

And with that, once again, all conversation ended.

When we got to the ski area, Sam parked. We all got out and grabbed our skis from the back of the SUV.

"We'll meet y'all back here about four," Sam said. He put his arm around Allie, and they started trudging up the hill.

"So where should we go first?" I asked.

"How about we ride on the gondola? To that restaurant at the top of the mountain? I could use some coffee and something to eat."

Even though he'd eaten more than his share of French toast and bacon. That was cool.

"Okay."

We started walking toward the gondola lift.

"Listen, Allie—"

I came to an abrupt halt and faced him, my teeth gnashing. "It's *Kate*. Why do you keep forgetting?"

"Ah, babe, I'm sorry. Like I said before, it's just confusing because Sam was talking about you so much on the drive up here."

I really didn't get it.

"Why in the world would Sam talk about me?"

"I guess because Joe was asking so many questions about you."

*Huh?*

"Joe was asking questions about me?"

"Yeah, you know. Stuff like does your sister have a boyfriend, what does she like to do?"

Joe had been asking about me? Joe who claimed that he was hanging around with me because I was the only one without someone? Joe who had a poker face that had allowed him to bluff Aunt Sue time and time again when we played Texas Hold'em?

Joe who had no doubt bluffed this morning on the back deck. And I hadn't called him on it. I'd folded.

No wonder I always lost at poker. I gave up way too easily. But I didn't want to lose at love.

"You know, Brad. I have to go." I patted his shoulder. "I left something back at the condo."

"What?"

"My boyfriend."

"But Sam said you didn't have a boyfriend."

"Well, as hard as it is to believe, sometimes Sam doesn't know what he's talking about."

# *Chapter 23*

*I*t seemed to take three hours for the shuttle that ran every thirty minutes to finally arrive at the resort. As soon as everyone climbed off, I got on board and dropped into the first empty seat.

"Quitting a little early, aren't you, little lady?" the bus driver asked.

"Just getting started," I said.

He gave me a funny look—probably because my words made no sense to him. But they made plenty of sense to me. I think I was going to finally get started with this amazing winter break.

The shuttle bus arrived at Snow Angel Valley and I got off. I started walking up the street toward the condo. I walked past A Novel Place, thought about dropping inside and talking to Aunt Sue.

But I didn't think she could offer me any more advice.

She'd once told me that she needed more than good looks and being nice to fall for a guy. And I'd naively asked her what else she needed.

She'd told me that I needed to figure it out.

I think I finally had.

What I needed was really simple.

I needed Joe.

When I got to the condo, I unlocked the door and stepped inside.

He was exactly where I knew he'd be, sitting on the couch, watching TV.

He glanced over at me.

"What are you doing back here?" he asked.

"So you were just hanging around with me because I was the only one, huh?" I asked, as I unzipped my jacket and draped it over a chair.

He shifted his body as though suddenly uncomfortable. "Yeah, that's right."

I sat on the couch. "Then why did you ask Sam so many questions about me while y'all were driving here?"

He directed his attention to the TV, just like he had that first night, a bit embarrassed maybe.

I realized that maybe he'd been crushing on me the way I'd crushed on Brad. Only I'd given up on Brad . . .

I was hoping Joe hadn't given up on me. Although I wouldn't blame him if he had. I thought Sam was clueless? I was definitely the winner in that category. Hands down.

"Look, Kate. We were just making conversation. It's a fifteen-hour drive and we made it without stopping. I was just trying to make sure that Sam didn't fall asleep."

"By asking him questions about me?"

"Don't read more into it than there is. We'd covered every other topic. You were the last thing we had in common."

He realized his mistake too late. His poker face caved, his cheeks turned red.

"What did you have in common about me?" I asked. "Other than you both knew me?"

He shook his head. "I didn't know you, Kate."

He looked at me then.

"But you wanted to know me?"

He nodded. "Yeah, I thought I did."

"You thought you did? Does that mean that you don't want to know me now?"

"I think I know you now."

"And?"

"Sam was right."

"About what?"

"He said that I'd really like his sister."

Talk about a surprise.

"Sam said that?"

"Yep."

Sam had actually said something nice about me, on a long drive. My brother was really a dope for making me think that he wouldn't say anything good about me to anyone.

But the best thing was that Joe agreed with Sam. Joe liked me. And I really liked him.

"If I call Aunt Sue and ask her to give us a ride to a place where we can rent snowmobiles, will you go snowmobiling with me?"

"What about Brad?"

I placed my hand over my heart. "My Brad-ectomy didn't even scar. What I felt for him was so superficial. I'll admit that this morning I was jazzed that he was finally showing an interest in me . . . I mean, it's what I thought I wanted. But it took me all of two seconds to realize I'd made a mistake. Brad wasn't who I wanted to spend today with. I wanted to spend today with you. Let me break you outta here."

He grinned. "I'm definitely down with snowmobiling."

"I can drive it," Joe said.

"I'd better drive," I said. "You're too doped up on pain killers."

"I haven't taken any since last night," Joe said.

Telling Joe that I thought we should go on a snowmobile outing had done wonders to improve his mood. Or maybe it was just that I'd chosen him over Brad. That I'd come back for him. And Aunt Sue, in matchmaking mode, hadn't minded at all giving us a lift to the rental place.

So now we were here, and Joe was balancing on one leg. He said that as long as he was careful, he could go without the crutches. Not sure the doc would agree, but who was I to argue?

Joe was a big boy after all, knew his own mind. And I was tired of playing nurse. I was ready to move on to other things.

"The controls are in the handles," he said. "I can drive."

I straddled the seat, took hold of the handles, and glanced back at him. "I can't believe you'd rather hold handle bars than a girl."

He angled his head thoughtfully. "I hadn't considered that."

"Maybe you should."

He hopped over, gingerly swinging his bad leg over to the other side and settled down behind me on the seat.

"You got rules on how I can hold you?"

"Nothing distracting while I'm driving," I tossed over my shoulder, meeting his gaze. "We don't need another accident."

"And when you're not driving?"

"The Kate-have-a-good-time fund is running low. Maybe you should think about making a deposit."

"Are you offering me a pity kiss, Kate?" he asked. "Because you still feel guilty about my bummed knee?"

I slowly shook my head, then I nodded. "Look, Joe, I do feel guilty about what happened. I can't help it. It was my fault. But my taking care of you, and maybe a kiss . . . they aren't connected to the guilt."

"What are they connected to?"

I swallowed hard and whispered, "My heart. I think."

Joe grinned, an absolutely beautiful, confident smile. He scooted up an inch and put his arms around my waist. "Drive, Kate. But when you stop, I'll be taking over."

Smiling, I nodded. I revved up the engine, wondering how long I could drive before the anticipation of his kiss would force me to stop.

I'd driven a snowmobile before. I mean, when you spend a few weeks every winter around snow, you start to explore the options other than skiing. I'd always ridden solo, but never alone. Someone was always on a snowmobile riding along beside me, usually Aunt Sue, sometimes Sam. I didn't believe in going out into the vast, cold wilderness without a buddy.

But going with Joe was different from anything that I'd ever done before, and not just because he was pressed up against me. I liked having him with me more than I'd ever liked being with anyone else.

The thudding of my heart that had been missing on the ride to the mountain this morning?

It was there now.

The awkward silence?

It wasn't there.

There was a perfection, a contentment, a joy that I felt just being with Joe.

Every now and then, I'd feel him loosen his hold on me and he'd raise his hand, pointing at something: a snow bunny that had suddenly stilled, waiting to determine if we were friend or foe; tracks where a deer might have wandered; or the way snow had settled into a drift that created an interesting shape.

We weren't just traveling through the forest. We were exploring, and I was looking at things in a new way. Looking at Joe differently as well. The way he was always there for me. The way that I wanted to be there for him.

I came to a stop at the edge of an ice-covered lake. I turned off the engine and listened for that awesome quiet that Aunt Sue had talked about that night we got pizza.

Imagine a place where there are no engines,

no motors. You don't hear the sounds of any gears turning or people talking. All you can hear is the thump of your own heartbeat. The release of your own breath. You're intensely aware of everything surrounding you, especially the guy who has his arms around you.

Joe kissed my neck and I was amazed that once again he'd somehow managed to find a tiny spot of bare skin. Then he kissed my chin, my cheek. He moved his hands to my hips and squeezed gently.

"Turn around, Kate," he ordered quietly.

The moment of truth had arrived.

I had to stand up and turn around and sit back down in order to face him. I wasn't exactly pleased with the results. Joe had long legs, his injured leg outstretched, so I couldn't get very close to him.

As though reading my thoughts, he grinned, put his hands beneath my knees, and pulled me toward him until my legs were resting on top of his. I was now close enough to drape my arms over his shoulders.

I couldn't figure out why, that first after-noon when the guys had arrived, that I hadn't taken one look at Joe and completely forgotten about my interest in Brad. Because Joe was definitely better-looking.

And nicer.

And sexier.

Even out here in the great outdoors, with an injured leg, there was an intriguing quality to the way he studied me. He wasn't an invalid. He wasn't weak. He didn't need a nurse.

And maybe that was the reason he'd gotten frustrated with me.

Because he wanted me to be with him, not because I had to be. But because I wanted to be. And I definitely wanted to be. Which he must have surely realized now, because like he and Aunt Sue had both told me—I was no good at hiding what I was feeling.

I wasn't sure when he'd removed his glove, but he trailed his bare finger around my face, where cap met skin. And there was the tingling—all over—so different from when Brad had touched me.

"I'm trying to figure out how much I need to deposit into the Kate-have-a-good-time fund," he said.

"It's pretty empty. You might have to make a substantial deposit." I couldn't believe how breathless I sounded, like I'd been running beside a snowmobile instead of riding on it.

His grin grew. "I'm still strapped for cash."

"You're torturing me, you know that? Did you take lessons from Sam?"

"I'm torturing you? Geez, you've been torturing me since the day we got here."

"Because I was interested in Brad?" I asked quietly, apologetically.

"Because you weren't interested in me."

"That's not completely true. I was interested, I was just . . . confused for a while."

"And now?"

"I'm not confused anymore. I know what I want."

"Me, too. What I've always wanted since I first saw you."

"Why didn't you kiss me again after that first time, that night on the deck?"

"You didn't give me any hints that you wanted another one."

I wiggled up a little closer to him and looped my fingers behind his neck. "What would a hint entail?"

He held my gaze. "Exactly what you're doing."

"Then why aren't you kissing me?"

He touched his nose to mine. "It's cold out here. What if our lips freeze together?"

"I'll chance it."

He kissed one corner of my mouth, then the other. I slid my eyes closed, waiting, waiting . . .

"Kate?"

I opened my eyes.

"You have the prettiest eyes. That was the first thing I noticed about you the first time I saw you."

"Where exactly was that?"

"In the hallway outside Sam's room."

I shook my head. "I'm sorry, Joe. I don't remember."

"No reason you should. There was a group of us coming back from supper. That's when I spotted you. You were laughing. You looked so happy." He touched his thumb to my cheek. "So pretty."

He put his hands on my waist, brought me a

little nearer, then he kissed me, and I was happy again, happier than I'd been in a long time. Because he knew my name, remembered me, was interested in me, thought I was pretty.

A girl likes to know that a guy thinks she's pretty.

I tightened my hold on him. He drew back.

"Is the fund full yet?" he asked.

I grinned. "Not even close. But when it is full, then we'll go to work on filling up the Joe-have-a-good-time fund."

"I'm already having a good time. A great time actually."

Then we were kissing again.

That night Joe and I went to the Avalanche with Sam and Allie. While Sam and Allie danced, we guarded the table.

"Hey, guys," Leah said, as she and Ian joined us.

"Hey," I said.

"So I heard this rumor that Brad and Cynthia broke up," Leah said.

"Apparently."

She studied me, dropped her gaze to the table

where Joe was holding my hand. She raised her eyebrows. "Something else happen today that I need to know about?"

"Nothing I can think of," I said. I looked at Joe. "Can you think of anything?"

He shook his head. "Nope."

"We did go snowmobiling," I said.

"Oh, yeah?"

"Yeah. We saw lots of wildlife."

Leah grinned. "And were *you* wild?"

"What happens in the forest, stays in the forest," I said.

Leah laughed.

Sam and Allie came back to the table and sat down.

"Did you see who's here?" Allie asked, pointing over her shoulder.

There, at a far off table was Brad . . . with Paige. Talking, laughing.

"That's an odd match," I said, smiling. "A bookseller with a guy who thinks *reading* is a four-letter word."

"Think he'll be packing up and moving in with her?" Allie asked.

I shrugged. "It's not really any of our business, is it?"

And the truth was, I really didn't care one way or the other.

"So, mates, anyone up for a game of darts in the back room?" Ian asked.

And the conversation drifted away from Brad and Paige. And actually everyone else drifted away to the back room for that game of darts.

Leaving me and Joe to once again guard the table.

"If you want to go play darts, I can hobble back there and watch," Joe said.

"I like being right where I am," I said.

"It doesn't bother you seeing Brad—"

I pressed my fingers against his mouth. "I'm totally over Brad."

I moved my hand away and shook my head. "That's not entirely accurate, because there was really nothing to get over. I thought he was cute. I wanted him to notice me. But it wasn't like I had any sort of real emotional attachment to him. So read my lips. He is so not on my radar anymore."

"Think I'd rather kiss those lips."

And he did just that.

# Chapter 24

*G*irls Night Out.

It was Leah's idea, because quite frankly, we'd come here together for winter break and we really weren't seeing much of each other. And there was a football game tonight so we wouldn't have the guys' attention anyway.

And of course, where better to have a girls' night out than at Aunt Sue's.

We were all sitting cross-legged on a large mat on the floor. Aunt Sue had decided to go international on us, cooking us a traditional Ethiopian dinner, which meant serving yourself from a large community dish.

"How many countries do you think you've visited?" Allie asked.

"I stopped counting at twenty-five," Aunt

Sue said. "But I do have a map of the world on my computer, and I color in a country when I visit it."

"What do you do when a country disappears or boundaries change to form new countries?" I asked.

"I don't worry about it, Kate. The map is simply a tool to help me decide where to go next. It's not my life's goal to get it accurate."

"Well, after I move here, I'll be happy to take an occasional vacation with you," Leah said.

"You really think you're going to move here?" I asked.

Leah glanced around, then nodded. "Other than the fact that I absolutely adore Ian, there's the snow factor to consider. I love it. I love the cold and the sports. Ian is teaching me to snowboard now. It's awesome."

"So how'd a guy from Australia end up here?" Allie asked.

Leah shrugged. "How does anyone end up here? He came on vacation and didn't want to leave."

"He's legal, though, right?" Allie asked. "Isn't

he supposed to have some sort of permission to stay?"

"Yeah, he has a green card, but when I move here, I'm going to help him prepare to become a citizen."

"Cool," I said.

"I think so. I mean, that he wants to be a citizen."

"Who would have thought you'd hook up with a foreigner?" I asked.

"Could have hooked you up with one—but no, you weren't interested." She smiled. "So how are things with you and Joe?"

"Terrific." I couldn't stop myself from grinning. I figured I was probably blushing, too. "I can't believe that I spent so much time crushing over Brad and didn't immediately move on to Joe. I just love being with him."

"For a while Paige was totally bummed out that she didn't have a chance to hook up with him," Aunt Sue said.

"She had a chance at the party at the lodge. She was all over him."

Aunt Sue gave me this knowing smile. "According to Paige, she didn't have a chance.

Apparently, Joe told her that he was keeping his options open, not planning to hook up with anyone."

"Kate changed his mind. Good going, Kate," Allie said.

I scooped up some food. "You wouldn't happen to know Paige's real name, would you, Aunt Sue?"

"Delilah Delfino. Her friends call her Dee-Dee."

I was a little disappointed. I was expecting something to make me cringe or gag.

"I thought it would be something . . . worse," I said.

"She just never liked it, so when she came to work for me, she decided it would be fun to change her name to something that would work in a bookstore."

"Oh," Allie exclaimed. "I just got it! Like a good book is called a page-turner." She shook her head. "I can't believe I was that dense."

"You had your mind on other things," I said. "Like my brother."

Allie nodded. "Yeah. I definitely had my mind on Sam. I figure you and I can go see him at the university sometime."

"You can see him," I told her. "I'll go see Joe."

"Is that where you'll go to school next year?" she asked.

"I was always planning to. I don't see a reason to change those plans."

"So what are his kisses like?" Leah asked.

I felt myself blush again. "Can't share descriptions, because I don't want to hear about Sam's kisses."

A secretive kind of smile spread over Allie's face. I really didn't want to think about it, but I thought maybe my brother did have some moves after all.

"I'm not sure I'll ever get used to you liking him," I said.

"I more than like him," she said.

"Yeah, well, just so you'll know . . . he's allergic to saying the L-word out loud."

Her smile grew. "Not with me."

I was stunned. "You're kidding me. He told you that he loves you?"

She looked like someone who had just scaled a mountain.

"Wow," I said. "You and Sam are just full of surprises."

"What about Joe? Has he told you that he loves you?"

"Right now, we're still in the seriously *like* stage."

"Seriously *like* is good," Aunt Sue said.

Yeah, I thought. Seriously *like* was very good.

The football game was over by the time Allie and I returned to the condo. Joe was stretched out on the couch, Sam in the recliner. Without a word, Sam got up, took Allie's hand, and led her down to the basement.

Which left me alone with Joe. I hung my jacket in the closet.

"Do you need anything?" I asked.

With a little moan, he swung his legs off the couch, making room for me. "I would say just you but that sounds way too corny."

"I like corny," I said, as I sat on the couch beside him.

"How was girls' night out?" he asked.

"Nothing spectacular. We ate Ethiopian—

oh! I just remembered. You don't have to marry Paige after all."

"Didn't know I was even considering marrying her."

"You were going to marry her so we could learn her real name."

"No, I wasn't."

"Well, anyway, you're off the hook. I know her real name."

He gave me a wide grin. "Oh, yeah? What is it?"

I grinned back. He was in his sleeping clothes: sweats and a T-shirt. While I was still in my going-out clothes. I reached down and pulled off my boots so I could bring my feet up to the couch cushion. I snuggled up a little closer to Joe.

He put his arm around me. "What's her name?"

"What are you willing to pay me to find out?"

"What did you have in mind?"

I pressed a kiss to his T-shirt–clad shoulder. "I'm not real good at being seductive."

"Kate, you don't have to try so hard with me.

Just relax. Everything will happen when it's supposed to."

I wondered what he meant by *everything*. And if I wanted everything with Joe.

"Delilah Delfino," I announced.

He made a face of disgust. "You're kidding."

"I didn't think it was *that* bad. Aunt Sue said her friends called her Dee-Dee."

"But she changed her name, because she didn't like it?"

I shrugged. "Apparently. Thought it would be fun to be someone else I guess."

"Man, I can't see me with a Delilah or a Dee-Dee."

"How 'bout with a Kate?" I dared to ask, my heart pounding as I waited for his answer.

Sometimes when you're trying to tease or be flirtatious you say something and as soon as the words leave your mouth, you wish you could draw them all back in. Or that you could back up a few minutes and stop the words from coming out to begin with.

That was how I felt at that moment. Like I was suddenly insecure in his feelings toward me. That I was seeking confirmation that he cared for me. Even though he'd shown it in so many ways, always being there for me when I needed someone. Standing up for me when I was laying out rules. Telling my brother he was being a jerk when he was a jerk. Helping out at the shop. Talking with me. Not blaming me for his wrenched knee, which definitely, no matter how I looked at it, was my fault.

Joe took hold of my hips and drew me onto his lap. He threaded his fingers into my hair, looked into my eyes.

"Yeah," he said. "I can see me with a Kate."

Then we were kissing. He was so good at it. He'd kiss me for a while, then pull back, look at me, smile, and kiss me again.

It was during one of those moments when he seemed to take as much delight in looking at me as kissing me that I said, "I really think you should sleep in my bed tonight."

"Kate, I'm not going to kick you out of your bed."

I nipped his chin and gave him a daring smile.

"Who said anything about kicking me out of it?" I asked.

\* \* \*

"What do you want to do today?" Joe asked.

I was sitting on his lap, on the deck, a quilt wrapped around us. The cocoon of warmth was heavenly.

Snuggling up against Joe was heavenly, too.

We were watching the sun come up. We always got up really early and came out here to watch the sunrise. I loved starting the day in Joe's arms.

And okay, part of it, too, was because I didn't want Sam to discover us in bed when he came upstairs for breakfast. After all, Sam still thought I was clueless about who was sleeping in his bed. He didn't need to know who was sleeping in mine.

And truly, who a girl is sleeping with is no one's business except hers and the guy she's sleeping with.

And Joe was totally okay with how I felt. He knew I wasn't ashamed of him or us. It's just that some things should be private.

I'd actually gained respect for my brother because he was keeping things private as well. Especially since it involved my best friend.

So now I was sitting here, snuggled up

against Joe, trying not to think about how few days we had left to be together.

We'd already started making plans to get together over spring break. But that sounded so incredibly far away—another time. Definitely another place.

"I don't know," I said. "Whatever you want to do."

"My knee's feeling better. Maybe we could just go walking. Do a little shopping."

"Shopping? A guy who likes shopping? You're a girl's dream guy come true."

"I was thinking you need a bathing suit."

"A bathing suit?"

"Yeah. I really want to take a dip in the hot tub before we leave."

I nuzzled my cold nose against his warm throat. "I don't need a bathing suit for that."

"No?"

I shook my head and nestled my face in the crook of his shoulder. "How 'bout tonight after everyone else goes to bed?"

"I'm there."

I sat up and kissed him.

"And until tonight?" I asked.

He gave me a devilish grin. "We'll think of something."

And I knew that we would. We'd ride the gondola up to the highest peak and have lunch at the restaurant at the top. We'd visit with Aunt Sue and sip hot chocolate.

Maybe we'd even go snowmobiling again.

We'd tap life on the shoulder.

And fall a little more in love.

$\mathcal{F}$or more wintery romance, turn the page to check out

# $\mathcal{I}$cing on the $\mathcal{L}$ake
## BY CATHERINE CLARK

*Cold feet, and hands, and ears . . .*
*but warm hearts!*

$\mathcal{S}$ top. _Stop!_ I commanded my skates.

"Look out!" I cried, seconds before I nearly smashed into a group of boys. Instead, I opted just to fall onto the snowbank, my legs crumpling beneath me, landing on my hip and lurching backward. _Very smooth, Kirsten_, I thought. Could I go home now? I'd had about as much embarrassment as I could take for one morning.

"Come on, girls," one of the boys said as he skated over toward us.

"Sure, where are we going?" my friend Jones (whose real name is Bridget, but no one calls her that) said under her breath to me as she helped me up from the ice. "I think I could follow _him_ just about anywhere."

I fought back a laugh. Jones was right:

Official Rink Guy, whoever he was, was extremely cute, but he also looked like steam might come out of his ears at any moment.

Then again, we were *all* sort of steamy, which sounds sexy, but wasn't, because it was only due to the fact that it was 12 degrees outside—and *everyone* steams in that cold. Dogs' breath can be seen from a mile away, especially when they're sled dogs running across the frozen tundra—

Okay, so this wasn't Alaska, and this wasn't the Iditarod—it was just Minneapolis, Minnesota, on your average late-December day.

And it was a gorgeously sunny day, which meant it was *extra* cold. We were at the park near my sister's house, which happens to have a huge cleared skating area, as well as a couple of enclosed rinks. The lake had some scattered ice fishing houses, which looked strange to me—the last time I was here, I'd hung out on the beach and built sandcastles with my nephew Brett.

The rink guy still stood there glaring at us with disapproval. He had a whistle on a chain around his neck, and he was wearing a red sports-team type jacket with the name Sean stitched on the front, sort of like a varsity letter jacket. Sean—I liked that name. He had blond hair, brown eyes, and was seriously tall. But then everyone looks taller on skates. Anyway, he didn't look cold in the twelve-degree, wind-chill-of-five weather. He wasn't even wearing a hat or gloves.

"Be a little more careful, okay? That's all I ask," he said.

"Careful? We are being extremely careful," Jones replied as she brushed snow off my back. (The good skaters *never* have snow on their backs.) "Have we killed anyone yet?"

"No, but there are lots of little kids skating here—I don't want anyone to get hurt," he said.

"But if the adults get hurt, *that's* okay?" Jones said.

He smiled, and his whole face went from semi-tough-looking to very-gorgeous. "You're funny. But no. That wouldn't be too cool, either. Just take it easy. Don't do anything crazy, okay?"

He shook his head and skated off to rejoin his friends, or should I say, co-skating-rink rule enforcers. They were circling the skating area as a group, as if they were the rink police of south Minneapolis, on the lookout for skating crimes. I kept my eyes trained on Sean for a lap. Watching someone that comfortable on his skates really impressed me. He was skating so fast, completely in control, and he looked good doing it, too. He had to be an awesome hockey player.

"He's very good-looking, but he needs to lighten up," Jones complained as she, too, watched the guys skating around. "Hasn't he ever seen people play Crack the Whip?"

"Maybe it's not a big thing here," I suggested. "Maybe there are different rink rules or something."

"Yeah, well, 'Crack the Whip' does sound a little . . . iffy. Doesn't it?" Jones asked.

"Iffy how?" I asked.

"A little sadistic. That's all I'm saying."

I punched Jones lightly on the arm.

"Look at Emma," I said.

She was doing a spin, and the guys that we were watching had stopped skating to watch *her*.

"She's taken!" Jones pretended to yell across the ice, her hand cupped around her mouth. Then she sighed. "It must be difficult to be gorgeous and talented."

"Let me tell you about it," I said.

"Ha!" She laughed.

We call our friend Emma "Emma Dilemma" because everything eventually becomes a giant problem with her—even the tiniest, most inconsequential things, like what to order for lunch or what shoes to wear. She's beautiful and sweet and has a tendency to be undecided, which is a bad combination because she always has some boyfriend or other pining for her while she goes out with another guy because she thinks she should give him a chance, too.

She constantly comes to her friends for advice. It can drive you nuts at times, but she makes up for it by being really nice and thoughtful. She never forgets important days for you, she's always bringing little gifts, and donating her slightly-used clothes and shoes (and boys) to charity—meaning me and Jones, because Crystal, who completes our group of four, has a serious boyfriend.

Crystal, meanwhile, was tilting her face to the sun, hoping to feel some warmth. Crystal had a gigantic winter coat that always made me think of Kenny on "South Park"—it's orange, with a big cone-like hood around her head that looks like an old diving helmet, only it has fur around the edges.

"Come on, Kirsten. Let's do it again!" Emma skated over and took my hand.

"We probably shouldn't. Those guys keep watching us," I said.

"They want to watch us? Let's give them something to watch," Emma said with a grin. "Come on, Crystal!"

The four of us got into a line, and somehow I ended up on the end again. "Hey, no fair," I said as we started to skate, faster and faster. Soon we were catching up to the guys.

Then my friends let me go.

I was like that battery bunny. I kept going, and going . . .

And I couldn't stop. And then I was crashing into . . . all of them. Two of them went down onto the ice and I landed right on top of one.

"Are you okay?" one of them I'd fallen onto asked, his face turning red, and getting redder and redder the longer I stayed flattened on top of him.

Then someone else kind of wrapped his arms around my waist and lifted me up. "Didn't I tell you to be careful?" I looked over my shoulder and saw that it was Sean. His hands were warm as he touched my skin — my jacket was short and my shirt had come untucked from my low-rise jeans — and he wasn't even wearing gloves.

"S-sorry," I stammered, as he held onto me for a few seconds longer than necessary.

The boy I'd landed on top of — who'd valiantly tried to stop me — got to his feet and asked, "You okay?"

"Fine," I said. "Sorry. Really sorry about that."

He shrugged. "No problem." I watched as he skated away. He was nearly as good on his skates as Sean — who was still holding onto my arm. "Just don't let it happen again," Sean said, "or we'll have to show you how it's really done." He gave me a little squeeze as he pushed me toward my friends.

*Good grief,* I thought. It was almost worth falling again.